BROTHERS IN WHALESONG

Brothers in Whalesong

Spirit Voyager

R. DE WOLF

Rhythmic Weave Books

A catalogue record for this book is available from the National Library of New Zealand.

Soft Cover ISBN 978-1-99-118960-8

Published in New Zealand
by
Rhythmic Weave Books
An Imprint of R. de Wolf
PO Box 438
Gisborne 4040

First Printing, 2023

Other Books by R. de Wolf

Guardians of the Ancestors

- Book One of The Spirit Voyager Series

The Future Weavers

- Book Two of The Spirit Voyager Series

Poetry In a Pear Tree

- An accessible book of poetry and reflections for everyone

The Goodness Algorithm

- Evolutionary Dystopia

Poetry In a Pohutukawa

- Reggie Reflections

In loving memory of my father
Pine Tamahori Amine Ngarimu
whose cheekiness and humour
inspired a whale.

Chapter 1

The Call

My whale brother, Ira, fills my mind with images of feeding in murky depths. In my sleep, I navigate the ocean as a whale in its element, and I burn with a yearning I don't comprehend until I wake startled as if yanked from my mat. The ocean whispers on the salt-laden breeze, *"Kai, we must go."* So, when dawn colours the clouds, I go to my parents' whare (house).

"I leave on the next tide. I cannot tell you why, but destiny pulls me."

My mother, Marama, searches my face sagely, understanding but unable to mask her pain. Starman, my father, clasps me to his chest and I can now look over his head. He is tall, but I am taller. We are both navigators, sons of the sea, and my father understands well the currents which drive our lives.

"You can't travel on an empty stomach. Come and eat with us. Your brother and sister will be upset you are leaving while they have to stay at home." My mother raises a brow, smiling wryly at the impending ruckus my departure will cause.

I agree, but leave to pack my gear before returning to my childhood home. Once I completed my manhood rites, I built a whare to give myself some privacy and space. To the villagers, I appear solitary but happy. The truth is, I am rarely alone as my connection to Ira usually ebbs and flows like the tide. However, we have remained together during the last cycle of the stars. I'm not sure if my yearning belongs to Ira or if his desire is mine.

Our meal is delicious, my mother's cooking is legendary, and the company is lively. My sister Aroha and my brother Maui are constantly locked in a battle of wits. It's entertaining, so I know I will miss them.

"Who will referee your contests when I'm not here? I ask you to spare our poor parents and stop this bickering when I leave the whare."

I ruffle their hair, but they are smart enough to know I am asking them to do this as a favour. Both give me a long blink, our secret code for agreement. My mother smiles at me, and I wonder if she has known our code all along. Aroha begs our father and me to tell the tale of our journey to the islands.

The ancestors have told her of my impending journey, and she is kind enough to think of Maui, who doesn't know yet. I cuddle my siblings and agree to tell them part of the story because I don't know when I'll see them again.

"When I was a boy, our father's ancestral home summoned me to the islands. Starman the Navigator," I always call my father by his name when I tell the story, "the Chief, my best friend Koha, Piki, and Papa Whetu all set off in the voyaging waka. The vessel was fast. Once we shouldered the sadness of leaving our loved ones behind, we gave ourselves to the excitement of the voyage. I remember those golden days as some of the happiest times of my life. Starman allowed me to put my navigation skills into practice during the nights, and in the sunlit hours, Tāwhirimātea flew our waka over the waves.

The Chief schooled us in the arts of leadership, strategy and arms. Papa Whetu taught us when to fish, how to choose bait and the finer points of surviving upon the sea's bounty. Our minds were soon as fit and nimble as our sun-baked bodies. Ira travelled with us. He is so familiar with the currents that his guidance sped our progress. Within a few days, Ira led us to Rangitāhua (The Kermadec Islands), where our parents formally committed to each other. Starman took me to the sacred cave where my tīpuna shared the gift of generations of navigating knowledge with me when I was still in Marama's womb. I saw stars sparkle from the walls of the cave in the torchlight. Magic surrounded me as blood surged in my veins, and I swam in the ocean with the spirits of my ancestors. They prepared me for the trial that would await me when I became a son of the sea."

My siblings fix their eyes firmly on my face. It amazes me that they still enjoy the story when they've heard it so often. Our mother looks on wistfully, enjoying being together but sadly aware the family dynamic is about to change.

"Tell us about the sea cave!" Maui cried.

"Maui, we need to be patient and let Kai tell the whole story," said Aroha gently.

"But it's the best part," said Maui, wide-eyed.

"But when he meets the girl is my favourite bit of the story," pleads Aroha. Maui's bottom lip quivers, so she rolls her eyes with a sigh, raises her hands in submission, and mouthes "ok" silently at me. Aroha indulges Maui even more than me, and I'll miss her thoughtful kindness.

"So, we arrived on the beach near Starman's original village. Many years have passed since he was a boy growing up there. Starman took some time to remember his whanau and friends. I experienced his loss with him on that beach and grew closer to my mentor that day. Together we paddled an ancient waka from the shore, out past the break of the reef. Starman prepared me for the initiation ceremony he planned at first light. Tangaroa, however, made other arrangements. A swift current grasped our waka and propelled us past the reef's drop-off into the deep. Ira sang to me that I must be brave and prove my worth. Chanting ancient navigating songs, Starman relinquished me to the care of my sea father, although he didn't know what to expect."

Maui's eyes shine, full round moons in his face. He knows the plot well but leans into Aroha, cuddling against her body in the crook of her arm, holding his breath.

"I dived into the sea. Unseen forces manipulate my body, and I plummet like an anchor stone through the water. My eyes are open, but there's no sting of salt. No craving for air in my lungs, and I hang suspended in time. An enormous fish swims lazy circles around me before beckoning me to follow. It's unlike any fish I have ever seen, with rainbows for scales. 'Your guide,' Ira whispers to me."

I recall the stories our mother told us and wonder if this is my great-grandfather."

Maui covers his eyes with his hands and emits a yelp, knowing what comes next.

"My leg jerks in reaction. I look down to see an enormous tentacle twining its way from my ankle to my knee. The creature is massive, dragging me sideways away from my guide. Frantically, I try and prise the sucking tentacle from my leg, but it won't budge. Peeping out from the shelter of the reef is a moray eel. I summon Starman's guardian, a predator of octopus, to help me, and he obliges. My leg is suddenly released, but a cloud of drifting ink disorients me. Closing my eyes, I thank the moray eel who wends around my arm to convey his relationship with my father. As the water begins to clear, I spy shimmering rainbow hues in the distance and kick out after my guide. The fish seems to slow, and it lets me close the distance until I'm almost on his tail."

"Be careful!" yells Maui.

"The hammerhead shark rams into me from below. Once again, I'm disoriented and begin floating upwards toward the surface. Then boom! The shark hits me again, knocking me sideways, before pushing me down. My body aches from the blows, and my vision blurs, so I reach for Ira, and he begins to sing. The refrain runs through me, and I feel I'm singing with him.

A pod of chittering dolphins surrounds me. They pound the shark with their blunt snouts, encircling me in their darting embrace, warning the hammerhead to back off. To my surprise, the shark withdraws after taking several blows. The dolphins swim with me, then tow me to catch up with great-grandfather fish.

Up ahead, I can see a dark opening in the reef, and my guide swims straight in. I want to follow great-grandfather fish, but a black and white sea snake bars my passage. We hang in the water, eyeballing each other. I advise him I go to become a son of the sea, but he stares back at me and doesn't budge. So I tell the snake the story of my great-grandmother who summoned sharks with her blood, as I know sharks eat sea snakes. At the end of the tale, I reach for my diving blade. The snake darts back into the reef as I raise the blade to cut my finger, and I swim past.

It's gloomy inside the reef, so my instincts guide me in the dark. I trust in Tangaroa (God of the sea), and he rewards me with a glimpse of blue in the distance. The rainbow fish sparkles in a ray of light, and I know I'm going in the right direction. We are swimming gradually upwards. The light is becoming brighter, and as I round the last bend in the tunnel, I'm stunned."

Aroha's eyes are half-closed as she envisions the scene, and Maui nibbles on his thumbnail. I will miss telling stories to my attentive sibling audience, and I swallow the lump in my throat.

"The tunnel opens to a pool of blue so intense with colour that I think I've entered The Well of Tangaroa. Walls tower above, and the azure eye of the sky gazes down on the water. Sunlight streams from the heavens in dazzling sparkles to ignite the divinity of blue. I drown in nature's beauty and don't notice I have surfaced to breathe air once more. Off to the side of the well is a sandy strip at the cavern entrance. Reluctantly, I tear my eyes from the water as something draws me to the cave. Once I step inside – my life changes."

"How did it feel, Kai?" asked Aroha.

"My wairua (spirit) tingled with life and expanded, shining with colour. It's hard to explain."

"It makes sense to me because your wairua always looks like all the colours in the world to me," smiles Aroha. "Sorry I interrupted; please continue."

"Tangaroa adopted me as his son. Waves rippled through me, then outward through the oceans of the world. My brother Ira joined me, and Tangaroa gave us a shared kaupapa (purpose). Our blood will run forth through generations and ages as guardians of Tangaroa's children." I always pause when I tell this part of the story because I feel the weight of the privilege Ira and I bear.

"And now, story gobblers, it's time to eat with Kai," said Marama sternly.

Nobody argues about stopping in the middle of the story for a change, and Maui follows Aroha's lead, and she knows I leave today. The meal is fantastic and the food extra tasty, so an excellent time to tell Maui the news.

"Mama, I will miss your cooking while I'm gone. At night I'll dream of your stew and fat-basted birds cooked slowly over the coals."

"Where are you going, Kai? Can I come?" Maui asks hopefully.

"I'm going on a voyage with Ira, Maui. You can't come with us, or when Papa travels, Mama and Aroha will be without a man in the whare."

I have considered the best way to tell my little brother. He worships me because we do fun activities together. When I depart, he will have to eel, fish, hunt, paddle, wrestle and dive with the other boys his age. Maui is popular with everyone, so finding companions isn't an issue. In truth, his pride in me as an older brother makes me feel extraordinary. Perhaps Maui will leave a more significant gap in my life than I will leave in his. I rumple his hair, and we poke out our tongues in unison with a noisy "bhaaah!"

The tide calls my name, and my blood runs with the waves. It's time for me to depart. Aroha and Maui scrape the flowing tears from their faces as they endeavour not to sob. I try to be brave for them and speak of the stories I will share when I return. When my mother embraces me, I struggle to blink the moisture from my eyes.

"I know Ira will take care of you, Kai, and your fathers, but I'm your mother, and I love you. We will speak and think of you every day you are gone."

My father comes to my rescue, slapping my back and telling me how proud of me he is. Of everyone, he alone understands the seductive call to voyage we experience as sons of the sea. He honours me with a hongi (touching noses and sharing breath) and nods his head at my waka (sailing canoe). Papa helped me build my voyaging waka when the elders initiated me into manhood, so it's well-seasoned for travel.

"Last night, my grandfather visited my dreams. He wants you to wear our sacred pounamu (carved jade) because it always longs to return home. One day it will be yours permanently. Wear it with pride. It is imbued with our navigation knowledge and the spirits of our seafaring tīpuna," said my father, placing the pounamu around my neck.

The optimal time to launch arrives. I wave to my whanau on the shore, and Ira shows off by splashing his tail, excited that I have returned to the ocean. Tāwhirimātea (God of the wind) teases the tears from my lashes as I hoist my sail to harness his breath. Although I am a son of the sea, I don't neglect any of the other Gods. Complicated karakia (prayer and ritual) were completed with my parents and Aroha to curry favour with the Gods and ancestors. The waka is laden with so many blessings that I fear it might sink. I laugh out loud at my joke, and a playful wave slaps water in my face. The thrill of the journey ahead seizes me, and I whoop for joy as Ira breaches, inviting me to follow.

Chapter 2

Brothers Unite

Ira is a humpback whale and he is magnificent. We connected when I was in Marama's womb, but Ira has grown immensely in the past few years. So have I, but my stature is puny in comparison to his. Our progress is swift. Even though we fish and play, sometimes I ride on his back while he tows the waka.

"Are we in a hurry, Ira?" I ask.

Although our conversations occur in our minds, it's as easy speaking.

"I must arrive at our first destination at the right time, Kai. It wouldn't do for me to be late. What if I miss something important?" Anxiety lurks behind his question, which is so unlike Ira. While I don't understand his sense of urgency, I share it. "You feel it too, don't you?" Ira asks.

"I can feel something, Ira, but I don't know what."

"We need to find mates, Kai. Our sea father gave us a task. Strong and enduring bloodlines won't create themselves, little brother – we need to get busy. I eat and eat to grow larger to compete for the best mate to breed healthy calves. How are you planning to attract a mate? You are well past breeding age but haven't produced any young yet."

I attempt to explain to Ira that I have plenty of time to seek a mate, but in the end, I concede he has a point. Like my Papa before me, I attract many wāhine (women), but although I have dallied and enjoyed their attention, I never settle. Now that I think about it, I'm one of the few men of Kāingatipu my age who doesn't have children. Perhaps I'm waiting to meet someone as special as my mother.

"Don't wait for a Marama to find you. Your mother is one of a kind."

"I agree with you, Ira, but I want the mother of my children to be special. To accomplish our task, I need a mate who understands our world. She will be intelligent, sensitive, spiritual, fertile, with a sweet nature and beautiful, of course. What's so funny? I'm so glad I amuse you, big brother."

Ira believes me a dreamer who has no understanding of the feminine psyche. He might be right, but I cling to the ideal I have envisaged as his laughter bubbles through me.

The sun deepens the colour of my skin at sea, and my hair bleaches to a streaky light brown. During the intense heat of the day, I shelter under my woven shade and nap, confident that Ira watches over me. When darkness descends, I search the stars and steer the course as ancient memories flow. My blood sings with joy, for I am in my element where I belong. I recall the story of my parents voyaging together and Papa teaching Mama to read the stars. Ira has baited my hook, and I start dreaming of sharing the wonders of the heavens with someone I love.

"See, Kai, you want a mate as much as I do," Ira gloats.

As a voyager, I'm grateful that I love the taste of fresh fish. The waka is laden with supplies from my mother, but Tangaroa blesses me with tuna and kingfish, which I fillet to eat raw, dipped in seawater. Like the dutiful son I am, I eventually eat my dried seaweed and smoked kumara as both my parents instructed me to do. I curl up to nap under a sun-filled sky with a full belly.

The lurch of the waka wakes me. I can't feel Ira for the first time in days, and I cannot speak to him. We are disconnected. Whitecaps ride the choppy waves, and the sky is now an oppressive mass of angry clouds. I sniff the air and know a storm is brewing, but I also sense hostility and wonder where we are.

While I slept, we may have strayed into the area where my people defeated their enemies en route to Aotearoa. Ira is a colossal whale, but that doesn't stop me from worrying about him.

"Where are you, brother?" I call into the wind, but there is no response. The wind is building, gusty and malicious, so I pull down my sail before it shreds. My waka tosses like a seed pod on the water, and I close my eyes to consider the available options. Ride out the storm and hope the waves don't swamp my waka, or try and run before the storm as Starman once did, continue to search for Ira and hope he can lead us to safety swiftly?

A water spout spirals from the ocean to my right, then another to my left. Inside the spinning water, I glimpse a blur of ghoulish faces, and their ill-intent smacks me in the face as they grimace, anticipating revenge. They shriek, and cold fingers brush my spine. But I am a son of the sea. My parents are Marama, Starman, and Tane the Brave, so I do not cower or flinch from these wasted souls.

"I belong to Tangaroa!" I shout in defiance. "You have no power over me. Go back where you belong." The ghouls cackle a discordant response.

"We demand utu (vengeance) *for our lost souls, you insolent calf. Together we will peel your flesh from your bones and eat you."*

The spouts move in on the waka, but I am chanting, calling on my ancestors, hands stretched to the sky. I implore my sea father to protect Ira so we may fulfil our task for him. Lightning cracks the sky, and the smell of ozone surrounds me as a bolt strikes the second water spout, collapsing it into the ocean. The first spout is upon me and the prow of my waka lifts, sucked upwards by the revolving water. Thunderclaps and rumbles signal a warning to the ghouls, but they reach for me. I grab my whalebone mere. The weapon is made from the bones of Ira's tipuna and laced with protective spells.

"Think you scare me dead things," I hiss, "we have defeated you twice before." Perhaps it is risky to taunt them, but I have a true purpose, and they do not. An internal heat warms me. The sensation of the sun kissing my skin and aroha (love) burning fierce and bright. Tane shimmers next to me, his flaming taiaha (wooden striking weapon) slicing impossible patterns through the air. On my left side, flanking me, is Nani Aroha, my great-grandmother. She cradles a stone bowl in her hands and blows glittering specks into the spiralling spout. I brandish my mere and strike the water. The ghouls are already screaming in pain as the spout dissipates in a cloud of spray. A hand reaches for me from the collapsing structure but evaporates under a double blow from my mere and Tane's taiaha.

My spirit father shimmers for a moment. His pride washes over me in radiant waves as he salutes Nani Aroha, and I feel so loved. The journey to the next realm no longer holds any fear because I have tasted the spirituality that awaits me. Finally, I understand my mother's explanation of her battle with the yearning to be reunited with Tane and her Nani. She told me about it because she considers it a flaw in her nature that I might have inherited. Now I know Marama is attracted to the divine, as any mere mortal would be.

Inspired karakia of thanks flow from my lips as if I have trained as a tohunga (spiritual expert) my whole life. My thoughts turn to my missing brother, so I open my skin and let blood flow into the sea. I am worried that I still cannot sense Ira. The current takes my blood. Sharks circle but soon lose interest when there is no prey, but I follow the direction of the meandering thread.

"Tangaroa, our quest is yet unfulfilled. Please aid me in my search for Ira, the whale, for something is amiss."

The current takes the waka, and I hoist the sail again, imploring Tāwhirimātea to undo the mischief of his deceivers. Suddenly my waka stops. I peer over the side and perceive a large shape on the bottom of the seabed.

The water is shallower here, so I anchor and dive in, making for the shadow below. It's Ira, but he is just lying there. He needs to breathe just as I do and I'm concerned we've been disconnected for so long. I am desperate to wake him up, but he is unresponsive. Swimming to the surface to breathe, I try to come up with a plan to stir him.

Tane's flaming taiaha appears in my mind, so I clamber aboard the waka and unwrap my prized weapon. The taiaha was made for me by an artisan of considerable skill. While I'm reluctant to take such a fine weapon into the sea, it might be the only way to save Ira. I rub the weapon with an extra coating of fat to protect the wood before I suck in as much air as possible and dive to the seafloor. Leaning into the taiaha, I place the sharp blade against the softest part of Ira's skin, trying to cause enough pain to get a reaction. He still doesn't move, and I swallow my panic. His eyes are robust, so I decide to poke his bum.

It isn't dignified, but I don't want to damage under his dorsal fin, and I already tried biting his mouth. I pray to everyone that he won't poop on me. Causing Ira pain is something I never expected to do, but his life depends on me.

My throat constricts, tears well, "please," I plead, "I cannot lose my brother."

Whether my sea father answered my prayer or my lack of air created a link between us, I feel Ira. Kicking for the surface to breathe, I scream at Ira in my head to surface. I share the taste of salt air in my lungs, my relief at breathing, and finally, he stirs.

Diving down and swimming to his eye, I urge Ira to come up with me. He is sluggish, but our connection holds, so I recite a mantra, "swim to the air," to try and move him. Ira lumbers through the water, lacking his usual poetic grace of movement. When he breaks the surface, Ira breathes and becomes more alert. My relief swamps him, and he teases me.

"Ah! So you do love me."

"Of course I do, you lump of blubber!" My tears of relief and snotty nose underscore my declaration of love.

"Ow, my bum hurts," he moans.

"Sorry, Ira, but that was how I woke you up because I ran out of options. Forgive me?"

"I'll think about it," he jokes. "What happened, Kai?"

"The spirits who assailed us possess a powerful sleep enchantment. These are the same ghouls who tried to kill my mother when our people fled to Aotearoa. My grandmother and tīpuna wove many protections around Marama and me while I was in her womb. It is the reason I was less affected than you. We must give thanks to them and our sea father. If it wasn't for their efforts, I might have lost you." My voice breaks with emotion.

"Well, perhaps I forgive you, after all, little brother. Let's sing a song of gratitude together."

I clamber atop Ira's hulking form and lay flat against him while we sing. The contact with Ira comforts me, and I am grateful because the separation has left me shaken.

When the stars come out, I triangulate the location of the foul spirits, determined to avoid ever passing there again. Ira is hungry and consumed with feeding to grow. His excitement is infectious. Too bad there will be no females waiting for me when we arrive at the whale breeding ground. Still, I am content with our companionship and hold imaginary conversations with my whanau, so I don't miss them too much. Marama's gentle words guide me through karakia and ritual. Aroha's insightful comments and Maui's laughter sound in my ears, and I spend every night surfing the stars with my father. Life is good.

"We are almost there, Kai. Wait for me here."

Ira quivers with anticipation, creating a surge of mating urges in me. I wonder if it will be the same for Ira when I find a mate or if he knows how to shut me out. When he returns, I will ask him. For now, I am a captive of his desires. Mating is not new to Ira, but this year he is a whale on a mission to impregnate as many healthy cows as possible. Humpback whales are not monogamous, and Ira won't have any responsibility to raise his offspring. He wants to father many calves.

My feelings about their customs are mixed. While it would be nice to do whatever you please, I'm sorry that Ira will not share bonds as I do with my parents and siblings. He pointed out he has me, and through me, experiences whanau aroha. His carefree exuberance is contagious, and I wonder if it inhibits my desire to settle. Sleep isn't an option for me, so I decide to fish. It will give me something to do and something else to think about besides sex – I hope.

The fishing is frustrating and a great distraction. I hook one specimen after another that wants to fight on the line or is inedible. After throwing back a barracuda, a pufferfish and a stingray, I decide to keep an aggressive squid. The chewy texture will provide variety to my diet, and it tastes good with seaweed. Eventually, I tire and sleep.

A dream unfolds, and I stare at a girl floating under the water.

"Where are you?" she asks me.

"I am on a voyage with my friend Ira," I reply.

"Well, I'm not sure I can wait for you much longer." She sighs in exasperation.

"Where are you?" I ask her.

"Waiting for you, of course, exactly where you can find me."

She's beautiful, and I am desperate to know how to locate her. There is something familiar about her, and I wonder if she's my mate.

"I will come to you as soon as I can. Please, tell me how to find you?" My dream voice is urgent and pleading

"Nothing in dreams is ever that easy, Kai. If you are coming, you need to hurry." The girl looks sad, and her image begins to shimmer before disappearing altogether.

I jerk upright - awake. To commit the dream to memory, I repeat our conversation out loud several times. Marama would know how to interpret the words and meaning better than I, but she is far away. My lip cops a good chewing while I mull over the words. Dream messages are often cryptic, but this one seems straightforward.

Scratching my head, I lament that I'm in a hurry but have no idea where I'm supposed to go. Ira will return when he's ready. He didn't say how long his mating mission would take, and it's been two days already. In the spirit world, 'soon' could mean any length of time, so I try not to fret about sitting around in my waka doing nothing.

The girl haunts me. Her face appears when I try to sleep but also when I'm awake. I long for Ira to return and reassure me I'm not going insane because I am obsessed with my dream.

The stars offer me solace, but the moon laughs at my dilemma. Marama's namesake turns the water to shimmering silver, reminding me of the vanishing face.

"My duties are fulfilled, little brother. You seem to be in a bit of a state," says Ira.

"You took your time, Ira. How many offspring can we expect?"

"I can't be certain, but Tangaroa will be pleased with me. Now, what ails you?"

My dream and the message tumbles out to Ira in a garbled mess. But, Ira comprehends the significance of the strange visit. He tells me we need to hurry to the meeting place anyway, so we leave immediately.

"Ira, I don't even know if that is the right direction. What if the girl is in Aotearoa?"

"Sometimes, I forget that for all your seasons, you are still a calf. The girl told you to come, not to return. How many places have you visited besides Aotearoa?" Ira asked, patiently awaiting my answer.

"Well, not many. We stopped at Rangitāhua on my last voyage, then Starman's home island, and we visited relatives on two other islands," I stammer.

"So, if she is waiting where you can find her, it should be somewhere you know. You also mentioned she felt familiar to you. Who do you know on these islands? Do you remember any girls?"

Ira's reasoning makes sense. It's been over ten years since I journeyed to the sea cave.

"Surely, it cannot be the Dolphin Girl? The girl in my vision looked like a goddess, and she wanted me to come to her. When I last met Dolphin Girl, we didn't like each other at all. I get along with everyone, but she was the most infuriating person I ever met. That is why I remember her so clearly. She was arrogant, went out of her way to play nasty tricks and make me look stupid. A surly gap-toothed, spoiled brat of an overindulgent chief," I frown.

"Yet you remember her still. Time changes many things, Kai. Look at how much your appearance has changed over ten years, and mine for that matter. Two fine specimens of our species, if you don't mind me saying so," he laughs.

For my sake, I hope Ira is wrong about the girl's identity. However, his instincts are superior to mine, and I struggle to remember any other girls, although I try desperately. As we sail in the moonlight, I hope my dream doesn't turn into a nightmare.

Chapter 3

Rangitāhua – The Meeting Place

You have missed a musical feast if you have never heard whales sing. The sound reverberates through me, liquifying my bones until flesh merges into the ocean. I, stupidly, assumed the voyagers who like to stop between Hawaiki and Aotearoa named the Meeting Place. The name Rangitāhua is much older than we are. Ira tells me whales have met here each year since they came to exist. They share news from around the world, places we have never dreamed of, with their haunting singing. I am one of the few humans who have attended a whale gathering.

The privilege of the experience fills me with wonder. At this meeting, the whales speak of all crucial matters to them and our world. I will try and recount how Ira explained it to me.

Whales exist to maintain the balance of life in the ocean. They are caretakers, gardeners, and monitors of Tangaroa's domain. Whales consume enormous quantities of the tiny creatures in the sea, redistributing the nutrients through their digestive process when they defecate and pee. I feel embarrassed that I often make fun of Ira about pooing new islands and drowning fish. It turns out he is fulfilling an important function.

At the annual meeting, they discuss food supplies and how best to sustainably manage krill and plankton stocks. The cows assess the safety of breeding grounds, travel routes, and they incorporate the number of new calves into each pod population.

What I find fascinating is the whales are interested in all matters within, on, and around the sea. The fish stocks of species they don't eat are equally significant to them, and they are aware of what people consume when we don't consider it. We respect Tangaroa and the sea, but apart from what we catch in our hapu, I have no idea how many or what species of fish other tribes take. The whales know so much information I'm astounded. To be honest, I feel like an ignorant child in their company.

They appear to envision the impact of environmental changes before they occur. I wonder if they predict threats as they sense shifts in balance or draw conclusions because the whales observe so much. It reminds me of a meeting of leaders I once went to with our Chief, but all the whales participated.

The whale singing is beautiful, woven with positive opportunities as they plan for the coming cycle. When the meeting ends, each pod and whale leaves with a purpose. My body is still vibrating, and I cannot stop smiling. Thanks spill from my lips, a liturgy of praise to Gods and ancestors, for I'm truly blessed.

I replenish my water and supplies while Ira socialises with the whales. Now the singing, he tells me, changes focus to romancing the cows. Males who wish to mate weave intricate melodies together, and so the competition begins. Ira has selected candidates he desires as a mate already.

Once the female is ready to mate, she breaks away, and the chase begins, but many contenders will pursue her. Fourteen hopeful whales surge through the water in her wake, demonstrating her desirability.

It's a furious chase across the ocean, and the first challenge for the pursuing whales is staying with their quarry as only the strongest keep up. They jockey for position near the cow and try to intimidate each other by blowing huge curtains of bubbles, but need to ensure their efforts don't cause them to fall behind. There is also a great deal of bumping and pushing between the closest males to try and shove each other out of contention as they try and attract her attention.

For the last year, Ira has dedicated himself to his preparation. He is fast, strong, enormous, and thanks to our connection, he's cheeky and worldly for his species.

I'm not the only one who learned strategic lessons from my parents.

As he flaps his flippers and rolls his cumbersome body with sinuous grace, Ira snares the cow's attention. She races off again with a startling burst of speed, but four males maintain the chase around her. When she slows, Ira aggressively bumps the closest whale away before rolling his body around her, and she allows him to caress her. The female has chosen Ira as her mate – his dedication yields the result he wants.

The cave where my parents once stayed together beckons, and I easily find the path. It was here my ancestors bestowed their gifts of navigation on me, and the spirituality of the place makes my extremities tingle. Reluctantly, I tear myself away to check my traps for birds, just as my mother did years ago. A change in diet is always welcome, so I spend the night ashore, cook birds over a fire and smoke some to take with me.

Ira is extraordinarily pleased with himself when he returns, and I know he's triumphant as soon as we reconnect. While he will laud his superior mating skills over me, I'm pleased he's been successful. He's my brother, and Tangaroa chose us.

"Your turn, little brother," he laughs.

"Not so fast - I am curious. I want to know why whales swim onto the beach and die."

"They have earned the ultimate reward - to return home from where we came," he replies, wistful.

The information confuses me because I know they were all born here, in their breeding grounds in the ocean.

"Yes, little brother, you are correct. We are born here as calves in your ocean, but we take this form to exist and do our work. Ultimately, we all return to our home, to the stars that created us – what you call Matariki (Pleiades). When it is our time, we shed our earthly bodies and nourish the whenua and ocean. We gift to Papatūānuku, and the creatures of your world, a piece of ourselves – our mana. The essence of our spirit lingers after we are gone."

"Sometimes, Ira, I feel pretty ignorant."

"You are young people, Kai, with much to learn. But you are clever and creative, and some of you are greedy and aggressive. Those ghouls we met, for example," he says with a shudder. "Our task, mine and yours, are critical because man has hunted us for thousands of years.

We are already planning for your population growth and its effects on us and the sea. Humans are skilled hunters and voracious gatherers. The lands in the north are more heavily populated than the south, but they will come, Kai. They have travelled here many times already, and there is wanderlust in their blood as there is in yours. Marama's father probably came on such a vessel, but the sea claims many of their waka."

"How do we stop them?"

"We can't stop them, Kai. What we do is manage and rebalance where possible. My offspring and yours will play a part in that delicate exercise. There may come a time when each species will have to save the other. For now, I have krill to eat, calves to breed and a brother who must find a mate. Come, we must hurry."

Ira makes haste, often towing my waka along while I sleep. When the winds prevail, I work my sails to extract maximum speed and enjoy the exhilaration of skimming over the waves. My beloved stars taunt me in my solitude, but clear skies map my route with sparkling light. "You are what I love most," I shout to the night sky, "and I believe you love me."

The moon, amused by my declaration, hides behind a cloud. Even I don't believe myself. Suddenly, I am yearning for a woman I don't yet know.

"You are pathetic, Kai," I chuckle to myself as I catch a fast-flowing current heading in precisely the right direction. Besides the ghouls, the entire universe is determined to cure my loneliness.

"We're almost there, Kai. What do you need to do to prepare yourself to compete for a mate?" Ira asks the question with such gentle sincerity that I know he is concerned.

"Well," I ponder how best to explain human rituals to Ira, "I don't do anything. It's not our way to eat until we become large."

"Little brother, you have no mate. Even without our shared task for Tangaroa, I feel duty-bound to guide you to achieve success."

"But Ira, you don't understand. I have mated with lots of girls, and most often, they pursue me without any effort on my part." I shrug my shoulders with a grin, recalling my last fling.

"How many offspring do you have, Kai?"

"None that I know of but-"

"Then you have not been successful in finding a mate." Ira is exasperated with me, but he is endlessly patient and continues. "Imagine Kai, what you would do, if you were trying to make yourself the most attractive mate for a female?" Ira changed tack. "When your mother readies herself for a ceremony, what have you seen her do? And Starman, before he embarks on a voyage, he prepares himself for days. My point is that your parents are both adept, but they still dedicate many hours to preparation rituals. You, little brother, are ignorant and arrogant. When I seek to mate with a cow that all the other males want, I do everything to improve my chances. If I wasted my mating as you do, I would have no calves either."

It is the closest Ira has ever come to growling me. He is my best friend, wiser than I am, so I consider his advice. My parents do expend a lot of time and effort preparing themselves for any activity of importance. I remember Marama's meticulous care with her appearance on important occasions, her offerings and karakia. Starman's voyage preparations are legendary in their complexity. My father spends many nights consulting the stars, ocean, Gods, and ancestors, followed by food storage, ritual and karakia.

It pains me to admit Ira is right and I am wrong. Once I surrender to Ira, he reassures me he loves me and wants to help. I take stock of my appearance – salt-encrusted and unkempt. All my karakia have focused on the journey, so I need to make changes. To find and win the mate I desire, I must be worthy. The Gods and ancestors can aid me, but I have to seek their assistance.

"Now you are using your head," Ira encourages me. "There is an uninhabited island on the way where you can bathe and attend to your grooming," he says, slapping his tail on the water and drenching me in the process. We laugh together, and I start my spiritual entreaties in earnest.

The reflection in the freshwater pool confirms Ira's observations, for my hair is matted and wild. Starman binds his hair when voyaging, and now I understand why. My father combed and oiled my tangled, unbound hair when we last travelled here. He also cared for my skin, pared my nails, washed me, managed my diet and stimulated my mind along with the Chief.

Left to my own devices, I haven't employed the lessons taught to me as a child, and I look terrible. I unwrap the neglected gifts from my parents. Soap, a wooden comb, moisturising scented oils and a new woven garment, ornately adorned. While I haven't thought about how I will look on arrival, my whanau has.

Aroha has fashioned a necklace of shark teeth and pounamu for me. Although Aroha is young, she receives many koha (gifts) for her healing work, and I'm touched she has designed the piece herself. Her connection with the spirits imbues all Aroha's work with layers of meaning, and like my sister, the necklace is unique.

My scrubbed skin soaks up the oils like a sponge, burnishing my deep tan. I oil my hair to help tease out the knots with the comb. It takes a lot of time; it hurts, so my lesson is well learned, and I clean between my neglected teeth. The smell alerts me to the festering fish residing between them.

Once I'm clean, I realise how paru (dirty) I was and that I was the source of an unpleasant smell. I feel fantastic. My muscles are defined from the voyaging and swimming with Ira, so I take out my weapons to practice knowing I can wash afterwards.

Tane, my spirit-father, is with me when I practice. Sometimes I wish I could speak to him like Marama talks with the spirits, but his presence is reassuring. Even on the waka, I practice daily. The Chief has instilled a belief that I must maintain my relationship with my weapons – they are an extension of my hands and arms.

I flow through the set movements of warm-up, defence, and attack, before finishing with complex strategic fighting patterns. Tane is in my mind and body with me, enjoying the flex of thought and battle muscles equally. 'A thinking warrior' is how the Chief described Tane to me. He was younger than me when enemies attacked but already able to identify the battle shift to save the Chief and his village. It broke Marama's heart to lose him, but she avenged his death. No less a warrior than Tane, my Mama (mother).

The strange nature of my conception has always intrigued me. Tane's spirit petitioned Starman to possess his body, to be with Marama one last time, and they created me. So, I grew up with three parents and three siblings, including my whale brother. Thinking of my whanau makes me feel happy, and I have another swim before attending to my weapons. In truth, I have done a better job of caring for my weapons than myself. I imagine Aroha waggling a finger in the air to admonish me and laugh aloud.

The waka skips from the island's lee on the tide as eager to be upon the waves as I am. My hair is tightly bound, so I don't have to repeat the painful combing, and I faithfully promise I will groom regularly.

"Goodness, Kai, the fish that like dead things will miss your aroma! Perhaps you will attract a female of your own species after all." Ira has a wicked sense of humour. I'm often the primary subject of his jokes, but he isn't unkind and noticed my stink.

"You should have told me I smelled so bad."

"Some lessons are better learned for yourself. Besides, I didn't want to hurt your feelings. I already called you ignorant and arrogant, so if I added paru and smelly, you might have felt I was picking on you. Now, you are presentable, and I am proud to call you my brother. Keep yourself clean, and practice with your weapons daily. I'm going to scout ahead."

Ira has never mentioned my weapons before, let alone asked me to train with them, so I'm slightly alarmed. I never feel unsafe on the sea alone, even though I know some people live to raid and fight. While I enjoy my martial training, I didn't think finding a mate would involve those skills. My brother does like to stroke my scales in the wrong direction sometimes, so I cease worrying about imaginary problems. Instead, I close my eyes and daydream of my perfect woman.

"Where are you? You'll be too late, and I'll be lost," she sobs.

My eyes snap open. I must have drifted into a dream, so I shake my head to wake up. But I can still hear her voice, heavy with sadness and despair. It's just a dream, I tell myself, but her voice has afflicted me with pessimism, and I hope my voyage isn't in vain.

Perhaps the beautiful, sad woman isn't destined to be my mate. The thought brings tears to my eyes. I don't know who the woman is or why I'm so fixated on finding her, but I am a fish stranded in a rockpool of destiny. Friendly winds drive my waka over the waves, and I thank Tāwhirimātea for his benevolence as the coral cays of the island group appear.

Chapter 4

Relatives

I wait for Ira to return because if he is scouting; there's a reason for it. The magnificent sight of Ira breaching never fails to impress me, and his return cheers me up.

"There is a commotion on the island, Kai. Many guests gather there, and some are just arriving, but people are wailing and rushing around in panic. I fear it isn't the most auspicious time for you to present yourself, but there is no hostile behaviour, and we need to find your mate. My advice is to go ashore and speak to the chief. Hopefully, they will remember Starman's son."

As I sail my waka through the channel in the reef, I can see Ira's description is accurate. The village is a buzzing hive of activity, and several visiting waka are pulled up along the shoreline. When I land, nobody pays me any attention. There is a meeting in progress, so I take my gifts and move to the edge of the crowd. People have grown quiet, so I listen with everybody else. The chief's women are crying silently, and he is emotional but turns to address us.

"Friends and invited warriors, you have answered my call to visit our blessed shores. Alas, tragedy has befallen us. Today was supposed to be a happy day - the day when one of you won my daughter and joined our family. Two days ago, Kali the dolphin, my daughter's companion, disappeared, and last night, so did my daughter." The chief swallows, putting on a brave front, but the distress on his face betrays his feelings. "Instead of competing in the tournament we planned, I beg you to please find my daughter. The one who brings Wai home will be handsomely rewarded and become my son."

The crowd begins to shout and jostle. A stream of boys and warriors run to their vessels, to launch, paddle and sail from the island in haste. I scratch my head as I wonder whether they know where they're going. As usual, Ira was correct. Dolphin Girl's real name is Waimoana, but her whanau call her Wai, and I'm not keen to recover her. Patiently, I wait for somebody to notice me and take me to meet the leaders, and I cling to the possibility that the woman in my dream isn't Wai.

"Aren't you going to search with all the other warriors?" asks an elderly woman.

"Not yet," I reply, "I'm waiting to speak with the chief. Forgive my poor manners, kuia. I'm Kai, son of Starman and Marama. Many seasons have passed since I visited your village as a boy. I voyage alone in my waka, and the salt has encrusted my sense of protocol."

"I remember you and your whanau, Kai. Welcome again, and I will let the chief know you are here. Pare, bring refreshments for our guest," she orders before trotting off.

The coconut milk is refreshing, and I remember how much I like it. It isn't long before a boy comes running to fetch me. Although I appeared at an inconvenient time, the chief's woman is a relative of my father, and these islanders are polite people.

I'm greeted formally as a family member, call them Aunty and Uncle, and they brief me on the woes that have befallen them. Smiling girls set endless bowls of food before me, and my aunt instructs me to eat. My appetite is massive, so I impress her with my appreciation, eliciting a grunt of satisfaction.

"Your arrival is auspicious, Kai. Perhaps the Gods sent you and your whale to find Wai," said Uncle.

"I'm not sure about that, Uncle," I say, "Wai and I never really got along. But, as long as you don't give her to me, I promise we will join the search. What can you tell me of the events that occurred in the moon cycle before she disappeared?"

"Wai is no longer the little girl you once met, Kai. Suitors come from everywhere to win her, for she has blossomed into a beautiful young woman. If you do find her, we are positive you'll change your mind," said Uncle with a knowing smile.

My gut tells me that Wai is the girl in my dreams, but she isn't the girl of my dreams – just my luck. She is, however, a distant relative, and I am honour bound to search for her.

"The last moon has been a hectic and unsettling time for our girl. Although many young, handsome, or wealthy men have sought to win Wai's love, she has refused them all. It's become embarrassing for us. Your Aunt and I are determined to make her a good match, and we are desperate for mokopuna, so we decided to hold a contest. Wai wasn't pleased with our decision." Uncle paused to wipe away an errant tear. "We only want the best for her, but she is adamant that she is waiting for true love. At first, we indulged in her fantasies, hoping that Wai would grow up and make a happy match. Her younger siblings have families already, but Wai waits and waits for someone or something she cannot explain." He sighs, and Aunty sniffs, wringing her hands in worry. "We were concerned that Wai has spent so much time with Kali the dolphin and her pod that she has lost sight of human customs. Then Kali disappeared. Wai was so upset she stayed awake for long hours searching for Kali from the beach and at sea in her waka. We couldn't even get her to eat, Kai. Finally, exhaustion overcame her, and we left her sleeping here in our home. Last night Wai disappeared, and although we look, we can't find her."

Uncle's misery and sense of guilt are written all over his face. Wai likely decided to run away to avoid a man she didn't want, and Uncle knows it. Being separated from Ira for the first time, I understand Wai's distress at losing contact with Kali. She may have searched for her companion, just as I did. I wonder if that is why Wai visited my dream and urged me to hurry or if she hoped my arrival would provide a distraction.

Either way, I don't want to paddle off in a hurry going nowhere. I will ask Ira to help me locate the dolphins while I resupply the waka as I have no idea how long the search might take.

"Can I replenish my provisions before I leave? Most of the search party left in a hurry without any supplies and will return soon. The ocean is vast, and I have no idea how long I will be gone. "

"Of course, you are right." Uncle's smile is wan as he hadn't considered the searchers wouldn't find Wai in a day or two. Aunty hugs me, shedding tears on my shoulder. I am sorry for them. Wai's behaviour is typical of the girl I met years ago who mainly thought of herself. Admittedly, there are other motivations in play, and I have no idea which one caused the disappearance. My search for a mate involves visiting many islands anyway, so I can combine both searches into one quest.

Chapter 5

Lost Taonga

A bedraggled parade of disappointed searchers returns to the island by nightfall. I spend the night on land with my Aunt and Uncle. By the time I resupply and make repairs to my waka, the sun's rays paint the horizon in hues of red and orange.

Once my relatives remember how far I have travelled, they feel guilty about sending me off to search for Wai after providing only one meal. They implore me to stay in their fale with them. Knowing it will be too dark to see anything and waiting on Ira for information, I agree.

After the voyage, the company of other people is a welcome change, but the social interaction makes me miss my whanau. First, I listen, then tell some stories. I inherited my mother's oratory skills and soon capture an audience of wrapt listeners.

Among them are several pretty girls who tempt me with beguiling smiles. Ira's words of wisdom are still sloshing in my ears, so I behave myself and return to the fale to get a good night's sleep.

My dreams are disturbing. Mournful cries rise from an angry sea as I throw myself against rocks, trying to escape. Ira wakes me, concerned. I am saturated with salty sweat and wide awake in the pre-dawn dark, so I sneak from my mat to avoid waking everyone else.

The sea invites me to cleanse my body, and I begin a complicated karakia to enlist the aid of my sea father. By the time I finish, the village has stirred to life. Washed clean under the waterfall, refreshed and reinvigorated, I'm eager to be on my way.

Aunty stuffs me with food one more time. Who am I to deny an older relative the comfort of providing? I eat every morsel and lick my fingers until her eyes gleam with satisfaction.

Tūātea *(breaking crest of wave)*, my waka, grasps the tide with sleek timber, eager to be underway. The mood reflects my restless itch to begin my quests. I thought being on land again, being with people, would hold more appeal. Instead, Tangaroa's task has created a void inside me that demands to be filled.

Lucky Ira can turn up at the mating ground, find healthy cows and swim off. Alas, my creation of offspring is proving more complex. I often wonder if the Gods created us for their entertainment, and I shake my head laughing, for I'm sure they find me amusing.

Ira is quiet. He focuses on the search for Kali, but as he can't find her so he looks for her pod.

"I cannot find Kali, little brother. It disturbs me because we have met before and she is a lovely, sensible dolphin. I believe she is far from here, but I cannot fathom why she left Waimoana without telling her when she would return. They are bonded, just as we are, and rarely separate. The pod may give us information, but if Waimoana doesn't know where Kali is, it is unlikely they will. The ocean is vast, so this search may take time."

"Do you suppose they could be in danger, Ira? We recently experienced the divisive meddling of spirits who wanted to harm us. Could Kali and Wai be in a similar situation?"

"It is possible. Those spirits we encountered, however, started their evil deeds as men. Tane's killer, and Marama's enemy, just continued his pursuit and vengeance in the next realm. There could be people or other creatures involved. Dolphins and humans aren't loved by everyone."

There was truth in Ira's words. Aunty and Uncle spoke of Wai rejecting man after man. Any one of those men could have become angry and decided to act. If you wanted to hurt Wai or make her compliant, you could threaten Kali. Wai will do anything to protect Kali.

On the other hand, Kali and Wai could have plotted their escape together to avoid Aunty and Uncle's matchmaking. I hope this isn't the case because finding them will be challenging if they hide.

The sky is clear, the breeze is warm, and my beloved sea embraces us. No amount of gloomy contemplation can dampen the singing heart of a son of the sea upon the ocean. My morning ritual yields a pleasing result, so I entrust my navigation to the deities. They have more idea of where to go than I do. I rig my shade sail and curl up for a nap.

"Kai! Kai, I need you. You must help me. Please hurry or–"

I wake with a start from the pleading dream. The voice still reverberates, like a shell held to your ear, murmurs of the waves.

"I want to help you, Wai, but you must tell me where to go," I tell the sky.

For all my dreaming, I still have no idea how to find Kali or Wai. The distress in her voice is pricking me like Marama's bone needles. My urgency to make haste is roiling in my gut, but I must put my faith in my guides.

The dolphin pod has no information for Ira. They felt Kali's absence, and they searched for her when she went missing but with no result. The disappearance is perplexing to them as they can communicate over a distance.

Ira is worried for his dolphin friend, which in turn, makes me worry about Wai. Painful she may have been as a child, but we share blood, she has asked for my help, and I must answer that plea.

I share my theory with Ira that angry men, rejected by Wai, could be involved. He agrees that humans are often motivated by negative emotions. Marama's lessons have endowed me with a superb memory, so I regurgitate for Ira every grain of conversation I heard consciously or unconsciously on the island.

The villagers' tales of crestfallen faces, disappointment, resentment, and mutterings of the unsuccessful candidates confirmed the embarrassment Aunty and Uncle talked about. Many arrived confident, laden with wealth as gifts or muscular physiques, preened to perfection and planned to paddle away with Wai in their waka. Wai found fault with each of them. While her manners have improved, rejection was gently respectful according to the villagers; any refusal can be embarrassing.

Uncle counted over 50 offers made and declined by men from all over the Pacific. Aue! I try not to be amused by Wai's behaviour, but it makes me laugh. Fortunately, Uncle told me where each man was from and, regretfully, the amount of wealth he didn't receive. Their island village, while beautiful, isn't prosperous, and I am surprised they haven't pushed Wai into a match sooner. Some men may have expected refusal because they didn't have much to offer or were elderly. The more offers Wai rejected, the more famous she became, so a neverending stream of people turned up to try their luck.

Ira and I focus on the men most upset at being refused. We have an advantage because Ira can snoop at sea undetected, and nobody knows me. I'm a voyager who returns to the region of my father's birth to find myself a woman.

The truth is a perfect disguise. My brother is confident he will find Kali if he cruises the ocean at speed, but we will come together each day. We don't want to admit it, but the separation caused by the spirits scared us. It has rendered me more empathetic to Wai's dilemma, even though I don't want to be. If only I could tell her in the dreams to give me information instead of orders. When I dream of her, there's no dialogue involved. Maybe being alone at sea is affecting me.

Our first destination is a distant island group that neither of us has visited. Uncle lamented Wai's refusal of the man who arrived from there because his waka was so laden with gifts it appeared in danger of sinking. The delegation was sure they would seduce the reluctant girl, and her father, with their wealth and good looks. When Wai was unmoved and said no, they were furious. It was fortunate that many hopeful warriors were on the island, all in the same situation, or the warriors may have attacked the village.

When the stars emerge, I chart my course. My evening on the island allowed me plenty of time to speak with the navigators. It's common for us to exchange information when we travel. Many navigators aspire to make the voyage to Aotearoa, so they were all eager to speak with me. Some are envious that I've already travelled back and forth. The exchange of information was helpful for all of us, and I know exactly how to get to my destination.

Content to be on the next leg of my journey, I sing songs to praise the elements that guide my waka; my mother's moon namesake, the God and his winds, my sea father's salty waters, and my beloved stars.

Ira spies for me. He doesn't want to lose me to an inhospitable host for no reason, for we have much to accomplish together. I don't pose a threat to anyone as I travel alone, but I am always vulnerable on land. My best defence is a disarming smile and cheerful nature.

With that in mind, I greet the people out on the water before approaching the beach. They wave back with smiles but don't stop me, so I beach my waka on the sun-bleached shore. A gaggle of children forms an impromptu welcome party. I'm grateful to them because it means I can approach the village escorted by my new friends. I enchant the children with my introduction and a teaser for a story of my travels. The time I invest in the children will yield a handsome return as they run off to tell friends and family of my arrival. We are a lively party of laughter and camaraderie when we arrive in the village.

Smiling adults greet me more formally and offer me food and drink. I imitate their customs as closely as possible, and I'm studiously polite. All my body language is open to welcome questions. These are skills I've learned from Marama and Starman on our trading travels.

"You have come a long way. What brings such a handsome young man to our shores?" asks one of the women. Her voice is soft but conveys gentle authority. Keen eyes sparkle with intelligence, curiosity and she wears leadership as comfortably as her shell necklace.

"Well, my father wants me to find a worthy woman to provide him with mokopuna to fulfil his legacy." I raise one eyebrow, shrug my shoulders, and open my arms wide. "What is a dutiful son to do? He launches his waka and sets forth on a quest he doesn't yet understand. Other navigators I met spoke of their travels to your islands, so here I am enjoying your hospitality." My wry smile speaks volumes of how uncertain I am of where I should go. "It seemed a good idea to look far away from home first."

Lona, for that's the woman's name, graces me with a sympathetic look. It isn't uncommon for parents to send young men off on adventures. The usual cause is that the boy or man's parents believe that he needs to mature before settling down. I am satisfied with her interpretation of my circumstances because it means I appear even more pathetic in her eyes.

"My son recently went on such an errand. He came home with a red face and a bad temper after being refused by his chosen woman," she smiled.

"Oh. Was your son one of the many admirers of Waimoana? I have just left the commotion on that island." Lona inclined her head in affirmation. "In my humble opinion, you and your son have received a blessing from the Gods. Wai and I are distantly related, and I can tell you she isn't a very nice person. When we were children, she followed me everywhere, belittling and making fun of me, playing nasty pranks, and making me miserable." I pause to let Lona digest my words. "My uncle asked me to search for her, and I made him promise that if I find her, he won't give her to me. I'm looking for the woman I dream of, not one who gives me night terrors."

Laughing out loud, I can see Lona is amused. She is also pleased by my unflattering but truthful description of Wai.

"Will you join my son and me to share food tonight, Kai? Your tale may be what he needs to hear to lift him from his gloom."

"You honour me, Lona, and I thank you for your kindness."

"When the warriors wind the conch before dark, please join us here. Now come, I will show you to the guest fale."

When I meet Lona's son Viti, I am astounded Wai refused him. Not only is he handsome, but his physique is perfect, and his muscles seem to have muscles. I am suddenly grateful to Ira for chastising me regarding my self-care. If I were to compete with this man for a mate, I would be spending my nights alone. The encounter makes me so self-conscious that I promise myself I will eat better and exercise more.

I sit next to Viti during the meal and choose my moment to speak of Wai. When I repeat my opinion of her, he laughs and hugs me like a long-lost brother. His mother gauged his mood well, and I've provided a balm for his smarting ego. I doubt any girl or woman has ever refused him before, and I empathise with his anger at Wai.

"The Gods must have brought you here, Kai, with such news of my lucky escape," Viti grins. "I owe you paddle-brother."

"Does that mean if I'm unfortunate enough to find her, you will take her?" My hopeful but comical expression signals that I am teasing.

"I am sorry, Kai. I'm grateful but not stupid. You may take her and her finely sharpened tongue home to Aotearoa with you." His smile is sympathetic. "But come with me. On this island, there are many beautiful women to entertain us with their dancing."

While Viti was correct about the entertainment, I didn't find my elusive mate. Lona tells me she'll watch out for someone exotic, I'm welcome to return any time, and she's content Viti has recovered his cheerful nature. They are disappointed I leave so soon. But the restless sea pulls, and my unfulfilled quests sit heavily on my shoulders. Viti and his waka crew paddled out to sea with me to guide me toward the next island group, and when we part, I leave friends behind. Such is the life of a navigator.

Waiting in the deep is Ira, who doesn't have any significant news to share, and we depart, patiently scanning the ocean for clues.

When I reach the Isles of Friendship, I greet them with the gifts Lona and her people have sent. To repay me, she ensured my warm welcome. The food is delicious, the company light-hearted and worthy of the island name, and the unattached maidens throw themselves at me mercilessly.

Viti warned me not to choose one. Coupling one-on-one is a commitment, but if many women share me – it's just fun. It isn't a common custom, and I do my best to impress them with my prowess.

As the sun streaks into the sky, I am sated and exhausted. My giggling companions depart before it gets light, leaving me wondering if I have experienced a vivid sexual dream. The ache and smell of my body remind me it was real, so I plunge into the lagoon but return to the guest's fale to sleep. Ira's words ring in my ears, and I feel guilty about wasting time on meaningless encounters, especially when I had such a good time.

Again I haven't found the remarkable woman or any trace of Wai and Kali, although I have questioned the villagers thoroughly. The islanders didn't send a delegation to compete for Waimoana because they were sure she'd choose Viti. Since he returned, a few young men have set out to cast their net, but all return disappointed.

I spend the next seven days travelling from island to island. The welcome is warm everywhere I go as I carry messages and gifts between families. Each village presents pretty, eligible young women, and I navigate diplomatically through the introductions to avoid causing any offence. None of the girls I meet is the mate I'm searching for. I have no idea what I'm looking for, but I assume I will know when I find it.

My hosts resupply my waka, and I'm about to leave when an old navigator approaches. We shared stories and food the night before, and his directions will be helpful.

"Kai, you must be careful. The southeast wind blows today, and the currents run strong in the deep water. I've seen the flow from the lookout." He darts his eyes around and steers me closer to the water's edge, where we will be out of listening range. "Stay away from the Black Island-Walu. It's a dangerous place."

The navigator sketches a map in the sand, which washes away a few seconds later under an incoming wave. It doesn't matter because I've committed the map to memory.

"Why is it dangerous?"

"Walu is the home of an angry chief and tohunga, and it's black because it's wreathed in foul magic." He spits into the sand and makes signs to ward off evil spirits. "They live for war and raids. Many years ago, they lost one hundred warriors, including the chief's two favourite sons. Those who go there don't return. Rumours circulate that they eat the flesh of men. If the girl has gone there, you will never see her again. It's not the place to seek a woman either; they don't allow external matches. Steer clear of trouble Kai, and point your waka into friendly winds."

We share a hongi. My wairua is disturbed, for I know the story of the lost warriors well. Fate is pushing me toward the mortal enemies of my mother.

Chapter 6

Spirit Guide

The wind blows ill. I pause in the middle of the ocean to seek guidance from Tāwhirimātea, the God of the wind. Marama and Starman have endowed me with the ability to perform intricate karakia, and I utilise my skills to rally support for my quests.

Ira's comforting presence washes over me as I finish the ritual, and as we merge, I feel complete.

"I found a pod of dolphins who heard a cry for help from Kali, but they were unable to locate her. They are concerned and are searching for her as they fish. However, Kali is silent. It is unusual for a dolphin to be out of communication, but it is consistent with the disconnection from Wai. Because we just experienced this, I'm inclined to believe there is dark magic at work."

"The navigator on the last island I visited gave me a lead. I feel trepidation Ira because I know in my bones that we must go where he warned me not to venture.

Walu, the Black Island, is home to a powerful tohunga and raiders. He told me if Wai is there, she will never leave. The raiders lost one hundred men long ago, including the chief's two favourite sons, and these people may be cannibals. Ira, these people are the enemies of my bloodline. They killed my grandfather, Tane, and tried to take my mother. Our families seem destined to clash across the realms. Perhaps Wai refused a man who doesn't take no for an answer, or maybe as her fame grew, she became a desirable acquisition."

My brother and I agree that we must follow the path set before us. We need to settle on a strategy that won't result in either of us ending up in a pot or umu (ground oven). I am my mother's child, so I call on my ancestors to protect Ira and me. The result of my karakia even surprises Ira, and I'm left speechless.

"Those raiders are starting to annoy me. Too stupid to know when to accept their losses. Aue!"

The voice in my head startles me so badly that I almost fall overboard. I've never spoken with spirits or had them address me. Ira laughs at me.

"Little brother, surely an old child such as you cannot become a spirit guide now." His amusement bubbles through me like expelled air when I'm free-diving. I know who the voice belongs to, so I try and talk back.

"Nani, what a pleasant - shock." To my astonishment, my humour tints my thought, making Nani cackle, just as she used to when she was alive.

"I can see that. Luckily you have Starman's balance. I didn't come here to drown you or to go for a swim."

"How are you here? Why are you here? I mean, I'm thrilled to hear you, but I don't understand."

"One question at a time, boy. Your spiritual umbilical cord has remained attached to Marama all these years. It is unusual. But it may be because you connect her to Tane, and neither of them has ever wanted to let the other go. I am using the cord to reconnect with you again, as we formed a bond when you were in the womb. Silly of me not to figure it out sooner, but necessity inspires creativity, Kai. You called on your tīpuna, and we respond. Three times we have defeated the raiders and their ancestral spirits. Eventually, they will find a way to defeat us. We have decided to end the raiders' ruling bloodline for all time. It isn't a decision we take lightly, so we petitioned the Gods. They support us because if we don't defeat them, the blood feud will flow through the ages and upset the natural balance of the realms."

"But Nani, you are my mother's spirit guide, so although I'm excited to have you with me – what about Marama? Tane travels by my side."

"You are a good boy to worry about your mother. However, she has more friends in the spirit world than I do." Nani sounds a little annoyed but also proud of Marama. "She hardly needs me anymore, Kai, and I am becoming faint with boredom. So, for the moment, I'm now your spirit guide if you accept me."

"Of course I accept you, Nani."

"Good, that's settled then. Ira? You need to accept me too, as we will go into battle together."

"I'm not as hasty as my little brother Nani, and I have questions. Will you remain my spirit guide temporarily or forever? How will Kai's relationship with you affect our bond? Is my sacred knowledge secure from you and other less benevolent spirits? Can we speak in the space Kai and I inhabit rather than both of us entering the spirit world?"

His wisdom fosters far more caution in Ira than I possess. I need to learn. Marama's diligence saved her in the spirit realm on more than one occasion, and I should have asked Ira's questions. Nani is clever, and I don't want her to think I'm an idiot.

"We can speak where you are comfortable, Ira. It doesn't hurt a spirit to get out once in a while, and it's a sensible suggestion, thank you. I'm Kai's guide, so only he can make you privy to our conversations. If he enters the spirit world, Kai may choose to do so alone or with you. The bond the two of you share is for life. Consider me a guest in your whare for as long as you want me to stay. When we finish our battle, I will depart, and your bond will exist as it was before I came. You are Matariki's child, Ira, and we, the offspring of Paptūānuku, cannot understand your language. The knowledge entrusted to whales is sacred and yours alone. We only hear your voice when you choose to let us. Marama, Kai, and now me, answer your call. The only way a malign spirit can enter the fortress of your being is if you invite it in.

So, to answer your question, I cannot access or provide access to your sacred knowledge."

"And now I understand Marama better. She is undoubtedly your mokopuna," Ira laughs.

"The three of us will be a formidable team. We are the spearpoint of our offensive," she says.

Nani's confidence is infectious. Her excitement stirs our sense of adventure, but she tempers it with a warning.

"Together, we walk into the fire. The navigator is correct; it's dangerous. Three heads are better than one, so I propose debating our strategy. It may be prudent, Ira, for you to invite Tane into our plans and battles at times. The enemy defeated Tane physically, but he won the skirmish in the spiritual realm twice. Tane knows the enemy well, but the decision to admit him or not is yours alone, Ira."

My heart warmed. In the time span of my life ago, Marama, Nani, and our Chief argued and proposed various courses of action against returning raiders. They triumphed, and I'm determined to continue our family legacy.

The brief from Nani was thorough. The chief of the raiders, Kapanval, was distraught when his two favourite sons didn't return from a raid on a peaceful island. With his best navigator Starman, who he'd raised in his whare on board, Kapanval knew they weren't lost at sea.

Kapanval was furious and drove his warriors relentlessly to search for his sons and the 100 lost men.

Eventually, a war party came across Green Island, and Kapanval's grief and anger turned bitter. None of the other sons measured up to the potential of his lost favourites.

In his despair, Kapanval turned to darkness, and un-natural magic, plunging his people into a cycle of especially brutal raiding and embracing cannibalism as a way of life. Every practitioner of dark arts was invited or abducted by Kapanval to feed himself with their knowledge. He consumed their secrets before eating them to steal their mana.

Over time, Kapanval became the most feared man in the islands. The raiders' home, once a pristine island group, became permanently shrouded in dark clouds. They were rich with wealth beyond their dreams, but they lived only to spill blood and do Kapanval's bidding. Kapanval lost his life-long passion for waka-building and seafaring, preferring to stay on land to make blood sacrifices and predict the future. As dead and displaced ancestors wove a destiny of malign intent, the people lost themselves, and their human spirits suffocated.

The raiders fed off the rich pickings of waka bound to win Wai. Word of Wai's exceptional beauty, her relationship with Kali, the dolphin, reached Kapanval's sharp ears. His blood stirred for the first time since his sons died, and he thought about breeding another heir. He wanted a boy who was strong of body and mind. A thinker and strategist who could learn his craft. Someone to repay the debts to the spirits who aided his conquests, including the lost sons, who were as aggressive and competitive in the next realm as they had been in life.

The longevity of Kapanval's life resulted from his evil magic, but he wouldn't live forever. A girl who rejected everyone might be waiting for someone different, so Kapanval decided to take her.

The old tohunga raved about paths and grand designs - he'd eaten them all long ago. In Kapanval's view, a man forges his way in life, and the bolder you are, the richer you become.

The birds who spied for Kapanval located Wai's island and observed to learn her routine. Evil spirits lurked to show Kapanval what possibilities existed to snatch her on land or at sea. Wai's love for Kali was a glaring weakness in the girl's defences. If they took Kali, Wai would follow. Once they separated the girl and dolphin from the rest of the village, the abduction would be simple, and the spirits could possess sea creatures for long enough to lure Kali into a trap.

The plan was simple and effective. Kali was presented with the bait and chased her favourite fish. She was put to sleep with a mixture of toxins and secured to an outrigger by the raiders. Kali's communication with Wai and other dolphins was severed in her drugged state, leaving her friends perplexed and then frantic. Kapanval was cunning. Once they had put distance between themselves and Wai, they allowed Kali to revive a little during the night. Just long enough for Kali to plant a cry for help in Wai's head.

The girl moved soundlessly to the beach and launched her waka to pursue the dolphin. The communication was faint, but she knew the direction of the message, and it was the only indication Wai had that Kali was alive.

The bond Wai shares with Kali has honed her sonar ability, and she's a strong paddler, as at home on the waves as the dolphin. Wai pursues the raiders, leaving her sleeping family and village in her wake. As light suffuses the sky, Wai comes upon a tiny atoll and stops to collect fresh coconuts for the journey. Kapanval's men lay in wait, swiftly subduing the unsuspecting girl. They bound and gagged Wai, took her waka, and erased the signs of her struggle. Pleased with the ease of the task, the warriors paddled swiftly for home to receive the rewards their chief promised them.

The raiders easily deceived Wai, and her actions were reckless, but I understand the love that drives her. I don't want to admit it, but I would probably do the same.

"Yes, you would have chased after me if you thought I was in danger. And I am far bigger and more worldly than Kali," claims Ira.

"Young people are so impulsive at times," says Nani.

"Fantastic – now I have two of you to entertain instead of one. Lucky me!" I shout to the sky, shaking my head as I laugh.

Together, the three of us plunge headlong into danger. There's no point being miserable about the impossible task ahead, so we sing, fish and eat as we travel. Nani regales us with a neverending stream of tales. I didn't know the spirits enjoyed adventures, and I assume from the stories I've heard that they are usually aloof - prone to delivering confusing messages and prophecies, my understanding.

Ira enjoys Nani's company as much as I do. It's Ira that notices Nani's stories are strategic and entertaining. Nani offers up historical plans and plots to consider as we formulate our approach. I don't attempt to hide because Kapanval's creatures already know I'm heading toward the raiders' island – Walu. Ira lurks in the deep, but it's challenging to be inconspicuous when you're so large.

"Have you settled on a plan, Kai?" Nani asks.

"Yes, I'm going to visit the island and tell them of my quest to find a mate."

"You are so like your mother - fond of baiting the hook with yourself. What will you do if they want to eat you?"

"Tell them I taste unpleasant, Nani. Besides, I don't have a lot of fat to baste my flesh."

We enjoy our banter. "I know I need to be unthreatening and entertaining. Our enemies will observe me, but I also have you and Ira to spy for me. When we locate Kali and Wai, we can decide how to free them before you fulfil your task, Nani."

"It isn't much of a strategic plan."

"I agree with Nani Kai. The simple truth is effective for some people, but I believe it would be better if you have some value alive."

"What do you suggest?"

"Maybe if we don't stray too far from the truth, the tale will be convincing. Your mother told you your father was a gifted navigator who sailed with the fiercest warriors in the islands. You are following in his wake, hoping to find him, and increase your seacraft knowledge - his name is Starman."

Nani chuckles in appreciation, for Ira's story is more believable than mine.

"Perhaps you can also tell them that Starman amassed a fortune in rare pearls that he hid to give to you when you attained manhood. Unfortunately, you don't know where the pearls are. These people are greedy and will want to find the treasure – it's a game that consumes them. Kapanval also misses his best navigator. If you impress him with your skills Kai, he may take you into his waka as he did with your father. It's difficult to hide a girl and a dolphin without someone betraying something. They may not try to hide her at all, as you'll be at their mercy. I hope you have your mother's skill for deception when required."

"He does deceive himself quite often, Nani – does that count?"

I almost welcome my mission to Walu, if for no other reason than to escape being the brunt of Ira and Nani's jokes.

Chapter 7

Raiders

Nerves gnaw at my insides like hungry rodents at the end of a long cold season. My bravado deserts me as I paddle into the enemy's jaws. I close my eyes in karakia, reaching for my sea father, fingers trailing in his waters. Calm cocoons me as my mind tumbles lazily in a light-filled lagoon.

My sea father replaces the leaden sky over my waka with summer blue, and my muscles expand and contract, seemingly of their own accord. Tangaroa readies me for the task ahead and remembers the raiders once deceived Tāwhirimātea and used sea creatures for their designs - the raiders irritate him.

Endless paddling has endowed me with a wiry body and untiring muscles, but I've transformed when I open my eyes. My body has grown in stature, and I now possess the sculpted physique of a mature man. I flex my arms and shoulders, test the balance of my bulkier thighs, and find it's better than ever.

"Gifts, Kai, because you'll need them. Tane wants you to practice your fighting poses religiously. Nobody walks onto Walu without being tested by the inhabitants, and bloodletting is their favourite entertainment. Most of the time, they squabble and brawl among themselves, but visitors provide a welcome distraction and variety to their lives. You approach as a boy, but make no mistake, if you survive here, you will leave as a man," said Nani.

Ordinarily, her words of warning cause me alarm, but today I feel invincible. I'll do as Tane instructs and start my training immediately, knowing the raiders may challenge me on sight. No matter who watches over me, and regardless of which Gods support me, I must be ready to defend myself.

For the first time in my life, I might need to be the aggressor and apply the lessons I've learned from Tane, the Chief, and my mother. Marama epitomises the passive aggressor, and I decide to use her strategy of cunning and cast myself as the weaker party so I never underestimate my foes.

Although my body is improved, my personality is unchanged, and I sing as I paddle and hail the first people I see with a cheerful greeting. The response is suspicious and cold, like frost on a coconut, in the islands.

"Kia ora, friend," I grin.

"Greetings stranger - who are you? And what brings you to this place?"

"I am Kai, and I'm searching for my father, a navigator."

"Hmmm. Follow me ashore. We don't welcome visitors here without a reason or invitation. I will take you to speak with the head of the guard."

The man, who didn't introduce himself, thereby insulting me, deftly manoeuvres his waka, indicating I should follow.

Walu lives up to its reputation as an inhospitable destination best avoided. Navigating through a labyrinth of choppy channels in the reef isn't easy, and my guide doesn't wait or assist me. Most visitors would be left behind or sink on the coral and rocks, but I'm a son of the sea, so their first attempt to get rid of me fails. When my guide scowls at my beached waka, I smile and thank him for showing me the way.

"Hmmph," he grunts before spitting on the sand and stalking toward a rude-looking hut.

I sling my belongings over my shoulder, reluctant to leave them at the mercy of raiders, and hurry after him.

Three warriors occupy the hut, engaged in a throwing game. They ignore us for a long while until one of them lets out a triumphant whoop! Goods change hands, and the two defeated men shake their heads. The winner turns his attention to us.

"Who is this?" he asks without acknowledging me.

"Kai, a stranger, looking for his father, a navigator. He followed me through the evil teeth, Pita."

Pita looks at me for the first time and narrows his eyes, raking me with contempt.

"Kai, what a delicious name," he sneers, inviting the others to mock me with him. He knows everyone has heard of their cannibalism. "I suppose you want to talk to someone in our village?"

"Yes, I do. Perhaps my father is there, or somebody knows where he is."

I'm a problem for Pita. If my father is here and he kills me, my father might retaliate. But Pita is responsible for ensuring nobody makes it to the village alive unless they earned their passage. He also doesn't want to show weakness in front of his men.

"Tell you what, Kai; I will do you a favour. If you can defeat me at our throwing game, I will take you to speak with Kapanval's guard myself. To give you a chance, we will play the best out of three." He smiles at his clever idea because he's the island champion and confident he can defeat me.

"Thank you for your kindness. I do enjoy games," I reply.

It's the truth, and I've honed my skills against my family, including lucky Maui, who is favoured by the Gods, Aroha, aided by the spirits, and my fiercely competitive mother. While I've never played this game, I'll learn quickly, and I watch their last contest with interest.

The game is simple. Three small coconut shells are placed on a branch, and each player has three round wooden balls of different weights to throw at them. The coconuts are moved further away and placed at varying heights. The contest continues until one player fails to knock down as many coconuts as the other.

I watch the guards play seven rounds, but I will only have three to gauge the weight of the throwing balls and the proper technique. Pita hasn't elaborated on what will happen if I lose, so I assume he's waiting to tell me at a critical point in the contest.

To counteract Pita's gamesmanship, I begin a complicated karakia with exaggerated hand and eye movements. I've always enjoyed spending time with tohunga, my parents, and now with Nani. Seafaring people are highly superstitious, so I shamelessly exploit their fears and leave Pita worrying about what might happen to him if I lose.

Magnanimously, he allows me one practice throw. Unimpressed with his effort to allow me a fair contest, I perform karakia over each ball, open my skin, and let my blood drip into the sand as I mutter with my eyes closed.

The warriors are rattled by my antics. They avoid making eye contact with me, hoping that it won't affect them if I have a grievance with Pita. My first throw is wide of the targets, and I realise the balls are unevenly weighted. Each of the warriors possesses their own set of throwing balls, which they received when they attained manhood, so they've had years of familiarity with them. I'm at a significant disadvantage.

Before taking my second throw, I toss the wooden ball in the air a few times to watch its trajectory and ascertain where the subtle weighting lies. The coconuts are close, and I hit one down with my second throw.

"Well, it seems you're a quick learner with some skill," says Pita, grinning like a hungry shark.

"You flatter me. I credit that one to the karakia."

He is overconfident, so I play along by throwing the next ball too high. It hits where I was aiming, at the tree, so I know I have a feel for the second and third balls.

"Bad luck. As the guest, it is only polite to let you throw first."

The snickering of the men confirms his statement is a lie. Pita throws last against all the other men and obviously prefers it.

"That is very kind of you."

"He is about as kind as a sea snake," whispers Nani.

The island is woven with dark spiritual protection steeped in blood, but Nani and I converse as whales and, therefore, outside the realm of man. She chuckles, reassures me that she will even the odds, and confesses she loves cheating. The admission comforts me.

I step up to the throwing mark and toss the first ball from hand to hand for a moment, then high in the air. Every move I make is theatrical, an elaborate dance with death.

The coconuts clatter to the ground, and the men pat me on the back as if I have done well, even though none of them has missed such a close target since they were young boys. I play along, accepting the praise as my due.

Amused warriors move the targets further away until we reach the starting point of their earlier contest.

It is only the first game, so I miss a coconut, conceding an easy win to Pita. His swagger and laughing exchange with the men announce that Pita is more sure of himself than ever.

"You can go second in the next round, and I will throw second if we need the third game," he said, shaking his head and making faces at his men.

We commence the next round with the targets placed where I missed them. Pita is expecting a quick conclusion to our contest. He is wrong. Six throws later, I have not missed a single target, and we are reaching the point where any man can miss.

An unexpected gust of wind knocks Pita's ball off its line, presenting me with my first opportunity to even the match. The miss frustrates Pita, and he curses everything and everyone around him.

"Of course, if you lose, I will recommend that Kapanval shouldn't hear your story. A sweet boy like you - someone could send you straight to the umu – yum!" snickers Pita.

I wasn't expecting his threat so soon in the game, so I grin at him knowing he has conceded his advantage. The contest will come down to skill and perhaps the cheating of a spirit enjoying herself.

The first throw flies perfectly on target, slamming the coconut off its perch with a satisfying *thwack*. My second throw isn't as tidy, but it does the job, though the target teeters before toppling with a thud. I talk to the third ball, murmuring instructions –

"No enchantments are permitted in this game. It's a contest of skill," said Pita, now deadly serious.

"Excuse me, Pita, but I offer no enchantments, only karakia to the Gods who made our world. If it bothers you, I will stop."

His frown expresses conflicting thoughts. On one hand, he has forbidden enchantments and may have provided himself with an opportunity to overturn the result should I win. On the other hand, he has denied the Gods the reverence they expect, possibly inviting ill luck.

I inhale deeply, slowing my heart and reaching for the tranquillity of my father's lagoon on a sunny day. As my arm draws back, shadows envelop the last target in darkness. It doesn't matter to me. My wooden ball is reaching for the coconut – fibre to fibre, a product of earth to the seed of earth's tree, Tāwhirimātea caressed, and Tangaroa protected. The aim has nothing to do with my ability to see the target – I can feel it. *Thwack!*

"I think I'm starting to get a feel for the game now, Pita, or more likely, my prayers are heard by the Gods. You can stop humouring me now and play at your best."

Several moon cycles have passed since Pita was last defeated, and on that occasion, he had overindulged in a mind-affecting drink raided from another island group. He put his miss down to bad luck and a gust of wind. My hit, he attributes to dumb luck, so Pita is still confident, which suits me just fine.

The first three targets fall easily for both of us, but the next set gives each of us a fright as my third target teeters precariously, deciding whether to drop. A smug Pita experienced a similar problem with his first throw, and I sense the increased tension in his body.

Two more rounds are completed without either of us missing. The whooping of the men announces it's now a contest because we've thrown further than anyone else. People drift over to see what's happening. More pressure on Pita, and I hope some kudos for me from the village leaders.

A hush falls as I prepare to take my first throw. I quiet my mind and body before focusing on the targets and my plan to rattle Pita. Thwack, thwack, thwack. The coconuts tumble to the ground in rapid succession. Now I have the measure of the stone's weight and flight, the pattern of the onshore breeze, and my eye accustomed to the light; I'm enjoying myself. Although I've never played this game, my contests against my parents as a child have made me a formidable thrower.

"That's it, boy. At this rate, I won't even have to cheat," Nani chuckles.

The triple throw dents Pita's confidence, but he's an experienced competitor, so he calms his breathing and shakes the tension from his arms before he steps up to the line. The crowd holds their breath. *Thwack!* The first coconut flies from its perch. *Thwack!* Number two rolls to the ground. The air thickens like coconut cream with anticipation. The third stone flies from Pita's hand, and his aim looks good, but Tāwhirimātea blows a random gust of air. The third stone whizzes past the target, drifting slightly to the left and thumps against a tree.

None of Pita's men dares to applaud my win, but in the spirit of the game, Pita turns to me and slaps my back in acknowledgement.

"Well thrown. A good contest, and I will take you to the village as I promised."

"It was a good game, Pita, and I owe the God of winds my thanks. You are a worthy competitor, and I am sure I couldn't have won without the Gods' assistance."

My comments are humble, truthful, and in earnest, for I have no desire to make an enemy of Pita. I accord him the respect of a skilled elder, even though I've bested him.

News of the contest and the defeat of their champion has reached the village long before we arrive. True to his word, Pita takes me directly to Kapanval's guard and introduces me to Taka. While Pita is respectful of Taka, I sense fear in his demeanour.

"You are correct in your assessment Kai, and so is Pita – Taka is a man to be feared. He lives to fight and fights to draw the blood from his opponents," whispers Nani.

"Be careful little brother. Think strategically before you make decisions," said Ira.

I am tall, but Taka is enormous. He towers above me and regards me as if I'm his next meal, with bared pointed teeth. His appearance reminds me of a mako shark, and strangely the thought comforts me – for I know sharks well, and they are my father's creatures. The idea makes me smile, and I greet Taka politely with respect.

"State your business on Walu," he orders, spitting upon the ground – another insult.

"I'm searching for my father, a navigator. My mother didn't give me much information – but I know he collected rare pearls and navigated a waka for the chief of raiders from boyhood. My search led me to many places, but a navigator from another island believes he may be here, on Walu. I seek an audience with Kapanval because I was warned not to come here, but if I ventured this far, I must have permission from your chief to ask questions. So here I am."

The mention of treasures sparks a gleam in Taka's eyes. He's a raider and a greedy one.

"Winning a throwing contest doesn't grant you the privilege of speaking with our chief." He spat again.

"What do I have to do?"

"You must meet me in combat. If you survive, I will tell Kapanval of your quest." Taka bared his teeth again.

"I have paddled all day today and participated in the throwing contest – may I have some time to recover my strength and be advised of the rules of combat?" I don't hesitate, blink, or show any emotion.

Taka throws back his head and laughs, a raucous blaring of amusement at my request.

"Of course, pretty one. I wouldn't want to defeat a tired boy. Choose a second to assist you, and you get to select the combat place and our weapons. We fight until one of us draws first blood, and any wound is acceptable. If someone is maimed or dies from the wound, there is no reparation to the family and no other rules. ”

"May I drink some water while I decide?"

I take the advice Ira gave me. Fortunately, Taka is also confident and finds me comical, so I fuss like a girl over my appearance as I slake my thirst. Pita regards me warily through narrowed eyes because he was fooled by me earlier.

"As I don't know anyone here other than Pita – I choose Pita as my second," I announce cheerfully.

Shutting his eyes doesn't wipe the worried frown on Pita's brow. Being chosen as a second is a serious role with a stringent code, but he doesn't want to upset Taka. He is confident in the fighting prowess of Taka, but then a short time ago, he was sure of himself in the throwing game.

Pita's nod of agreement contradicts the angry stab of his gaze. Right now, he hates me, especially when Taka slaps his thigh in joy. I'm not the only person insulted today.

Placing my hands on my hips, I chew my lip as I mull over my options. It isn't my habit, but one I've observed when people can't make up their mind, and I want to appear indecisive. I've already run through my options, considered the pros and cons of each one, and made a decision.

The prudent choice is to play to my strengths, but I assume Taka can best me in combat. If we end up in a contest of strength, Taka will crush me. Weapon choice is critical. I can't just choose a spear, as I may find they have spears superior to mine. My mere is an old friend, but I don't want to engage in close fighting with this man. I stowed my matched daggers on the waka, which are familiar to me, but while I'm an excellent marksman, Taka may be able to throw further. He may draw blood from me before I reach my throwing range. I believe he won't like my chosen weapon, but the decision is mine. Ira and Nani support my decision.

"I choose our waka upon the open ocean as the combat ground and my short paddles as our weapons – one each."

Taka knows I'm seeking an advantage for myself, but he's a skilled raider with years of experience on the water. He acknowledges my clever choices, but he isn't intimidated. Raised in the most brutal settlement in the islands, Taka, is a survivor who fought through the ranks from humble birth to earn his position on Walu.

I don't dwell on how Taka rose to become head of the chief's guard, but I know he'll kill me if he has the opportunity.

"You may take a time of rest to recover your strength. I don't want my men to think I only defeated you be-cause you were fatigued from a throwing contest."

The men hoot with laughter and begin making bets. They don't bet on me, but how long it will take Taka to draw blood. Only Pita dares to place a small bet on me at ridiculous odds. I'm pleased Pita invested in me because I need every scrap of assistance.

"As Taka is the challenger, you will choose the way your waka will be facing. Although we don't have sunshine, looking into the light is still a disadvantage," volunteers Pita.

"What can you tell me of the currents, winds, and reef in front of the island Pita? Are there any areas I should avoid?"

"The tide is receding, and when it becomes low, the entire area in front of the island will be littered with emerging rocks. Eddies and channels form between the larger stones. Navigating between them requires a lot of strength, manoeuvrability and Taka knows the rocks like brothers. Allowing you to rest will give him the advantage. You must go far out into the ocean if you are to have any chance of surviving an encounter with Taka. He has a bad temper which can sometimes cloud his judgment, but I caution you not to provoke him because his skill is such that he's never been defeated here. If you toy with him as you did with me, your death will be slow."

Information is valuable to me, and I appreciate Pita providing me with a chink in the defences of the formidable warrior, even though he cautioned me not to be provocative. I ask Pita many more questions while Nani and Ira supplement my knowledge with their spiritual and undersea observations. My waka needs attention so Pita accompanies me to the beach. The design of my waka is different to the raiders and I ask Pita to point out the craft Taka will choose. There will be advantages and disadvantages with each of our craft and I need to consider how to exploit any advantage.

It has been a mentally challenging day so I take some sustenance from my own supplies including one of my mother's seedcakes and meditate to relax my body. Ira flows his strength into me and Nani marshalls the spirits to fend off the island's ghouls. To Pita's surpise I fall asleep snoring gently and dream of swimming in the waves of Walu. When I wake, Ira and my father's sea creatures have created a three dimensional map of the ocean in my mind.

I don't want to open my skin to make an offering to my sea father before the combat challenge, but I commit my blood to him. Karakia flows from mouth and fingers as I call on the Gods to support my vengenace on their behalf. Although I mutter and use a Maori dialect so Pita won't understand too much, his eyes widen as he perceives me as a tohunga.

By any standards, I'm young to be adept in spiritual matters but I began training in Marama's womb before I was born. My parents are deeply reverent and both have unique connections to the spirits and Gods. I never expected to receive the gift of spirit guiding after reaching manhood, and I'm thrilled Nani is my guide. Her aroha ripples through me as she reciprocates my feelings.

"We are a formidable team Kai, connected from the moment your essence formed. Taka is not invincible."

Nani's words comfort me but I don't let my confidence off its anchor. I fight for my life, so envision what I want that life to be. The girl from my dreams flits through my thoughts, as do the children I wish to father, an ocean of life with Ira, and my beloved whanau. With so much ahead of me, and to live for, my desire to succeed is a well-honed blade.

To maintain the illusion that I'm more concerned about my appearance than the combat, I oil my skin, dress my hair in a top-knot decorated with feathers, and flex my limbs in an exaggerated warm-up. My vanity isn't all a show – I'm enarmoured with my new bulging muscles. The laughter that drifts from Taka's men is exactly what I want to hear.

A warrior approaches Pita. From the corner of my eye I see them huddle together in conversation before Taka and his men depart. Pita strokes his chin thoughtfully as he wanders over to tell me what is happening.

"It seems the Gods do favour you. Perhaps your prayers were heard because you'll live to see another day. The chief sent Taka on an urgent errand, so the combat will take place tomorrow instead of today. It's a deviation from the rules of the challenge and I have negotiated that Taka must offer you hospitality – food, drink and shelter for the night. However, it is my duty as your second to ensure you remain alive and I counsel you to eat your own provisions and sleep under the guard of my men."

"My thanks and prayers are with you Pita – you are a man of honour. If you show me where I can sleep, I will heed your advice."

We return to Pita's men to fetch my belongings, and true to his role he organises a guard for me and my waka. The hut where I will sleep is crude and looks like it was built to house prisoners but they allow me to clamber up a tree for fresh coconuts. I'm hungry, so I eat, quench my thirst and to the surprise of the men guarding me, close my eyes to rest on my mat. After such an exciting day I'm tired but I also want to connect with Nani and Ira. The additional time to replenish my reserves is a boon I should use wisely.

"Well little brother, your foe heads away from the island at speed. I am following him because he goes to check on the girl they have hidden somewhere in the island group. It can't be far if he fights you tomorrow," muses Ira.

"Why is it urgent? She isn't hurt or anything is she?"

"Relax, the girl who you do not care for is fine for now. I managed to locate Kali. She was trapped in a stone crater. The raiders created a rockslide to seal the only entrance and threatened to kill Wai if Kali didn't stay quiet and cooperate. My resident small fish found a way in and I broke her out. Kali is hiding but will now be able to reach Wai, which is important because they threaten to hurt Kali unless Wai does what they want."

"So, they are worried that they have lost their leverage and that Kali may try to escape with the girl. What do they want with Wai?"

"I believe I can answer that now," said Nani softly. "Taka's men on the waka talk among themselves. Kapanval wishes to father a son with Wai so he awaits the crescent moon – the most auspicious time to conceive he has been told. Once he has the child, he will sacrifice the mother as a blood offering to the evil ones he worships. We don't have much time."

"Will they guard her where she is Nani or bring her here to their stronghold?"

"That's a good question Kai, but I don't know what they plan yet. Remember, Wai was abducted and everyone is looking for her. As formidable as they are, the raiders don't want to unite the rest of the region against them and secrets are difficult to keep when too many tongues are involved."

"Get some sleep little brother of the sea, for your father has more to show you of this island and the group, now we have time. You must defeat Taka tomorrow."

And I did sleep deeply in dream. The rumble of my snoring helped to keep the night guards awake and started whispers that I didn't behave like a man who was about to fight Taka and probably die.

They aren't sure if I'm too stupid and vain to realise Taka will kill me or if I'm more than I appear. Gossip circulates, fueled by Pita's men who witnessed the throwing contest and my karakia so furtive bets are placed.

Nobody wagers publicly against Taka but if I survive the ordeal there's wealth to be won and the raiders love gambling.

It's late morning before Taka and his men return. Ira now knows the location, and Nani observed the warriors imprison Wai in a cave. She's isolated on an island with no waka, but with Kali free, they don't want to risk Wai escaping to the ocean.

They leave their prisoner food and water but tell her nothing of her fate. Still, Wai is content because Kali is free and they reconnect. Kali doesn't know anything more than Wai but at least they have each other.

Pita and Taka's second reschedule our combat and Pita wrings every advantage he can out of their requested delay. I suspect Pita wagered more on me and I'm beginning to respect his negotiation skill. Taka will have the light in his eyes, and we will engage beyond the reef.

My preparations are more complex and completed to a new level of spirituality I didn't realise I possess. Perhaps my skills are newly acquired gifts. Our seconds inspect the paddles meticulously to ensure they are equal weapons. It wouldn't be fair if one had a sharp edge to draw blood and the other didn't. The seconds will accompany us in their own waka. Once a fighter draws blood, he yells "blood" and fighting stops while the seconds inspect the wound together.

The choice of weapon means I won't be speared, cut or stabbed and killed with one lucky strike, but it does mean I can be bludgeoned internally without drawing blood or knocked out to drown. I want to win, but I cannot afford to hurt Taka and deprive Kapanval of a favoured warrior. If I do so, I may be evicted from the island but will more likely be sacrificed or eaten. It isn't an even contest.

Chapter 8

The Contest

Each man launches his waka and navigates the reef. I have studied Taka's craft from a distance, and I watch carefully how he pilots it. Tūātea is heavier and faster at sea, but the opponent's waka is sleek. Any hopes they had of me sinking in the treacherous channel are dashed as I smoothly guide my waka as if I've lived here all my life.

We head to opposite sides of the channel in deep water with our seconds to allocated positions. As Taka is the challenger, Pita will call the start of engagement on my signal.

I stand still with my eyes closed and mouth open, feeling and tasting the movement of the air.

"Now!" I shout to Pita.

Tawhirimātea breathes life into my sails, and Tūātea flies like a cast spear directly toward Taka. The sun is directly behind me. He tacks to remove my visibility advantage. I study his waka and how it responds to his commands. It is fast and nimble. We feint, and circle one another as each of us tries to gauge the skill and weakness of the other. Taka searches for an opportunity to board my vessel and sails closer on each pass.

Pita specifically told me not to goad Taka, but I want to rile his temper and affect his judgment.

"I didn't realise you wanted a sailing contest," I yell as I zip past Taka.

I am rewarded with a murderous look for my effort.

"Are you tired from your errands?" I laugh at our next pass.

Taka doesn't react this time, but I see the tightening of his jaw as he clenches his teeth. As I pass Pita, his face is white with fear, and he shakes his head at me. When we turn this time, Taka sails his waka at speed, then turns straight at me. I see his thigh muscles tense and anticipate his leap onto my waka.

As he jumps aboard my waka, I land light-footed on his, take command of his sails and speed away – doubled over with laughter. Taka is apoplectic with rage. His face is an unattractive shade of crimson because he doesn't want to ram his own waka.

"Can't we just fight like men?" I goad. "I was tired of waiting for you, challenger."

I manoeuvre his craft adeptly and steal the wind from his sails, leaving Taka becalmed in my unfamiliar waka. But Taka is a sea raider, and he's soon moving again

– albeit a bit more clumsily than when I sail because Tūātea and I are one.

I sail and tack until I'm behind Taka with the wind at my back, calling on my sea father to aid my cause. He answers with a rolling swell that accelerates my speed at an alarming rate. My control of the vessel is minimal as it surfs to the rear of my waka.

Taka's fingers grip hard, trying to steer the waka to where he can see me. From the front of his waka, I lean out over the water and strike from behind with all my might and momentum at the thin skin of his knuckles - dangerously close to colliding.

The skin splits with the blow, and I scream "blood" as the rigged sail veers me away after scraping a greeting to Tūātea. Raising his hand in disbelief, Taka watches blood ooze from his knuckles, and our seconds sail to inspect my claim. After the initial shock at being defeated, Taka throws his head back and laughs.

I have won fairly and without inflicting major injury. Taka is a warrior, and he shakes his head in admiration of my strategic victory. He is magnanimous in defeat. They live by a strict code, so he pledges to announce my arrival to Kapanval and escort me to see the chief himself.

Pita is almost as pleased as I am, and I wonder what he wagered.

Before we depart for the shore, I open my skin with my knife and allow my blood to mingle with the sea in thanks to my father. As I intone karakia to the Gods, the men surrounding me experience tingling in their wairua. They realise I'm not the vain boy they mistook me for.

The path to meeting Kapanval has been risky, and now I must wait until he decides to see me. Taka sends me food while I languish in my hut. They permit me to attend to my waka, exercise and swim, but I'm not free to roam. I spend hours meditating, they think, but I'm actually with Ira and Nani. Ira knows which island Wai is being held on, but I'm no longer free to go and rescue her.

Nani has a plan. Now that Kali is free and can communicate with Wai, she can instruct the girl to escape with Ira to another island as long as Ira can bring them closer together. There are three pairs of warriors guarding Wai in shifts at the mouth of a cave with only one exit. It is up to Nani to help Wai escape and swim out to Ira.

We hope before long, I will have my audience with Kapanval. I will give Nani, and her spirit warriors access to the inner circle of power on the island, so they can plan to overthrow the ghouls and destroy them.

The rescue plan is in place, but my escape route from the island isn't clear. Kapanval, could send me on my way, enslave me, sacrifice me, take me into his service or eat me. The future is murky. Somehow, I need to convince him I'm more useful to him alive. I know he held my father in great esteem as his navigator and trusted him, so I plan to position myself as a potential replacement. I place my trust in Nani and Ira to be able to rescue me before vengeance is unleashed upon the raiders. But for now, I need to provide a distraction for Ira and Kali.

Two days and nights pass, but finally, Taka arrives.

"Kapanval will hear your request tonight. Try not to displease him." Taka nods at me and turns to leave.

"Wait!" I yell. Taka pauses, his back facing me. "Do you have any advice for me?"

"Do not lie to Kapanval. He always knows."

As Taka walks away, I mull over his words with care.

Chapter 9

Kapanval

A winded conch shell commands the torches are lit. Drumming erupts in a cacophony of beats, signalling the end of the day. I dress with care, as I've seen my parents do on many occasions. My body is oiled, I don my best attire, tame my hair, and line my eyes with cold charcoal. The light eyes I inherited from Marama, shine once rimmed with black. A unique curiosity to behold. Adding to my appearance is my defeat of Pita at throwing and Taka in combat – I am, at least, interesting.

"Yes, you are interesting, mokopuna," cackles Nani. "They whisper about you because you pique their curiosity. Your feats have reached the ear of Kapanval, and he's amused. These people are isolated, and they love a good tale. Give them what they want, Kai, and you'll win the night."

"Thanks, Nan. What will you be doing?"

"Pilfering their thoughts and knowledge to find a weakness. The benefit of connecting through Ira is that their spirits are unaware of me. I will also watch over you, Kai, and enhance your stories. Good luck."

Taka fetches me, and I follow him to the centre of the village, which is teeming with people. Almost the entire village comes to see what happens when I meet Kapanval. They know the infrequent visitors who do arrive, rarely depart alive, and it's been years since their chief saw a stranger. The guards lead me away from the crowd to a large pavilion.

Kapanval sits upon a carved dais, surrounded by gorgeous women, flowers, and he's flanked by two armed warriors. He must be old, but he doesn't look it, and his skin is white. There are no tohunga with him, so perhaps the rumours that he ate them are true. Only his eyes look ancient, strange, and grey, but red where the whites should be.

I open my arms with palms facing him so he can see I'm unarmed, and I bow my head in acknowledgement of his superior position. My friendly conversations have served me well, and I've been on many diplomatic missions with my father. Kapanval regards me frankly before speaking.

"Taka tells me you want to speak with me – so talk," orders Kapanval. His voice is raspy but booms out in the space.

I pause for effect, then look straight at him with my unusual, light-coloured eyes. There is no challenge from me, but also no fear as our eyes engage.

"I am Kai, from Aotearoa. My mother is Marama from the lost Green Island, and my father is a navigator and son of the sea – Starman is his name. My mother fled from her island home with her people before it was destroyed, and she told me Starman was your navigator. Is he here with you?"

My introduction contains no lies. The question is merely a question, but I'm grateful for Taka's advice, as I would have embellished the story with lies otherwise.

"No, your father isn't here," responds Kapanval.

"Do you know where he is?" I ask.

"No."

"Do you know if he lives?" I ask hopefully.

"No, I do not. Many years ago, he went on a raid with two of my sons and never returned. So, you have traversed the ocean for nothing. Are you a son of the sea?" Kapanval asks.

"Yes, I am."

"Is that how you defeated Taka?"

"Yes, my sea father aided me in our contest." Another truth that I hope will restore his faith in Taka, who I don't want as an enemy. "I was raised to revere the Gods and trust my life to the sea, and I couldn't have defeated Pita or Taka without karakia and assistance."

Kapanval considers me, a young man standing before him whose father, Starman, was the best navigator he's ever had due to his intuitive relationship with the sea. He took Starboy into his home, replacing the father killed by his men and his kindness was repaid by gaining an outstanding navigator for his raiding waka.

The only mistake Kapanval made was sending Starman on a raid with his two favourite but overly competitive sons. Kapanval wonders if the spirits have sent me to replace Starman. Still, he's cautious. While I seem honest, the timing of my arrival when the islands are teeming with search parties is a concern.

"Your father was raised as a son in my house, and I still lament the loss of my best navigator. Starman's son is my mokopuna. Come – my warriors join me to eat. Sit here, and you can tell me about your life," says Kapanval with a predatory smile.

His teeth are a dark colour, stained by the nuts used on some of the islands in ritual ceremony. It gives Kapanval an evil look.

"You honour me with your hospitality. Starman is not here – an unfortunate shame for me – I hope he still lives in good health."

I choose my words with care, so no lie falls from my lips, but my downcast eyes imply disappointment and fear to Kapanval, who assumes Starman died with his sons.

"You do have family here, navigator. Your father had three beautiful sisters, and the youngest still lives here with one of my nephews, so it seems we are family."

Kapanval highlights our familial bond for a reason. Good navigators are a valuable resource to seafaring people. The prospect of meeting my aunt and cousins is a welcome surprise, but I wonder what happened to my other aunts. Now isn't an optimal time to ask.

Nani's advice is put to good use. I tell amusing stories about myself and from around Aotearoa. Kapanval and his men appreciate the fresh material and my entertaining oratory skill. Fierce as they are, I manage to get them laughing with the hilarious tale of being fought over by three sisters.

At the time, I didn't find it funny, and I was embarrassed, but the spectacle of brawling girls pulling hair, scratching, and slapping each other amuses the men. I was just a boy at the time and had no interest in girls. The victorious sister emerged from the scuffle to find I'd gone fishing with her brother. Only her furious mother stood ready to punish her daughters for causing such a ruckus in front of guests.

As the night wears on, other people share their stories, so I listen avidly and participate by asking questions. I do my best to make friends with as many people as possible. Our party becomes louder and louder until a disagreement erupts, and Kapanval dismisses us with a wave of his hand. Taka escorts me to my hut.

"Thank you, Taka. I didn't find my father as I hoped to, but I did meet Kapanval as you promised, and I have family here - I am grateful."

"I believe he values you, Kai. You're a lucky man. Good night."

Nani ensures I rest well, and Ira lets me ride with him in my dreams while he feeds. I hear the urgent chittering of a dolphin, and then my dream girl is with me. She's so beautiful – surely she isn't Wai?

"Kai, where are you?" she pleads.

"I'm close now, and Ira, my whale brother has located the island where you are a prisoner," I reply, able to speak to the dream girl for the first time.

"The guards joke amongst themselves that their ancient chief wants to father a son with me, then kill me. You have to save me."

"Kapanval is waiting for the most auspicious time to conceive a son. I am on Walu with the enemy as I arrived here to look for you. Right now, I'm not at liberty to rescue you, but we still have time. You must come up with a plan to get to the ocean. If you can swim or paddle into the deep, Ira can spirit you away on his back. Now that Kali is free, you don't have to worry about them hurting her."

"What do you suggest, Kai? I'm guarded by at least two warriors day and night. Am I expected to fight my way out of here by myself?"

Her tone is cutting, so even in my dream, I know it's Wai. I remain peaceful because I have no desire to enter a nightmare of bickering with my childhood adversary.

"You have always been clever and resourceful. There is always a way to achieve the outcome we desire if we want

it badly enough. I will ask my spirit guide to send you inspiration-"

"You have a spirit guide?" she asks in disbelief, giggling. *"What's so funny?"*

"I never imagined spirits would talk to you or you to them. All you ever wanted was to be a son of the sea, and that's all you'd talk about - very boring."

"Well, I have an extremely skilled spirit guide." Nani's purr of approval soothes me. *"Focus on karakia, and seek assistance from your ancestors and mine. It's time to swallow your pride and humble yourself if you want to cheat Kapanval of his desires."*

I break contact with Wai. Subconsciously, I know it's my dream, and I want to have the last word. How is it possible for someone to goad you while you are sleeping, I muse before turning over to resume my rest.

I sleep late because the sun is muted behind the dark clouds over Walu. Kapanval hasn't released me yet, so I'm not free to go. One of his men arrives mid-morning to summon me because Kapanval wants to see my navigation skills for himself.

The best sailors have assembled to practice navigating the treacherous reef while their chief watches. Conditions are challenging, with gusty wind and a receding tide. It is an opportunity for me to impress Kapanval. I want to win more freedom so I can gain information and plan my escape. Kapanval watches as I launch Tūātea and join the procession of waka heading for the lagoon.

The chief languishes on a large log under a shade made of palm fronds while his women fan him. It's Taka who shouts instructions to us from his waka.

"Our chief has designed an obstacle course through the reef. You must collect each of the markers in the right order. First, a blue starfish in the small channel, then a green coconut from the large channel, orange coral from the wrecking rock at the mouth of the channel – then you must zig-zag back, collecting three different shells from each marker on the reef by a route of your choice."

Taka holds aloft an example of each of the three shell trophies. "To make the exercise interesting, Kapanval will award a prize to the winner - a rich prize."

Hoisted above his head in each hand, Taka displays a fine club and a matching spear. Each of the weapons gleams with years of oiling. The club tapers to a sharp point at the bottom to be used for bludgeoning and stabbing. A perfect enticement for raiders. "But that isn't all. Our chief offers the winner first pick of the dancers who will perform at our feast tonight."

A cheer erupts from the other competitors, so I add my voice to theirs. My mother would have something to say about how Kapanval treats women, and it wouldn't be complimentary. Nani chimes in for her.

"Aue! Another man who treats women as a commodity to be traded. Our female ancestors scream for a slow and painful death for him. You must be far away before the wrath of two realms descends on these fools. Kapanval made a blood sacrifice this morning Kai. He stirs his creatures to wreak havoc upon the course today. Be on guard for spiritual interference."

A smile lights my face because I know Nani is with me. It makes me look like the over-excited raiders. I feel like all I do on Walu is participate in competitions, and I thank the Gods I am good at it.

As we head to the starting position, I continue my karakia, tasting the wind and offering myself to the elements. There's a foul taint in the atmosphere, so Nani weaves a cocoon of wind God's breath around me. Tangaroa catches Tūātea in his currents. Sailing is easy, and I use the reprieve to survey the competitors, their craft, and how they move. Many of the craft are nimble and better suited to navigating the reef. If I complete the course and acquit myself well, there will be no doubts about my skill. I wonder if Kapanval sends his bloody disruptors against me or if all competitors will be challenged.

"He targets you, Kai. But, the other competitors will be caught in the foul winds and fickle currents as a consequence. I'll make sure of that," she cackles.

We turn our vessels and sail for the starting line, jockeying for position. I see a waka sailing hard to cut me off, and know my competitors work as a team. Tāwhirimātea fills my sails, and Tūātea leaps forward, propelled by the water. My speed is so high I leave the other waka in my wake. As I navigate the small channel, driftwood appears in front of me, seaweed drags at the waka, and the rest of the field closes in.

I run to the front of the waka and reach to claim a blue starfish suspended on a pole over the water, it sways out of reach against the wind, and I miss it.

"Tūātea, Tangaroa, Tāwhirimātea hold true," I plead as I run to the back of the boat and execute an impossible leap to snag the starfish. My waka catches me as I roll onto the deck, clutching my prize. The other waka are now right behind me, but the pole is swinging madly, thwarting attempts to grab one. One navigator uses a net on a handle to scoop his starfish, and another swings out on his sail. Navigators who innovate when conditions are unpredictable – my key rivals.

When I turn into the large channel, rocks have sprung up everywhere.

"They're an illusion, Kai," murmurs Nani.

Closing eyes I can no longer trust, Tūātea is guided by my other senses as my sea father navigates the passage by guiding my hands. The wind God brooks no interference from marauding ghouls, and they only succeed in hindering the progress of my pursuers. I copy the navigator behind me and grab the green coconut with my spear before I tack toward the wrecking rock.

It isn't called the wrecking rock for nothing. Protruding into the entrance of the large channel, the rock has a jagged line of teeth, and each one can punch a hole in a vessel. What you see above the surface and what is hidden beneath can change in a heartbeat. In addition, the current swirls around it in random eddies, impossible to predict. The coral tokens are unhelpfully positioned in the middle of the rock. None of us can reach the coral without wrecking our craft.

I'm drawn to my fishing line. I can throw the line far enough to reach the coral batons, but it's unlikely I can hook one from this distance. Casting my eye over the supplies, I find what I need. There is a sealed bowl of gummy sap for repairing leaks at sea. Starman never travels without it, and neither do I. Attaching a large flat clam shell to my fishing line, I smear it with sticky sap, chanting to the wind to help my cause. After a couple of pretend throws to gauge the weight of my shell, I let it fly, and it floats aloft on my prayers.

"Yes!" I scream as the coral sticks to the sap, and I reel the baton and shell in with a clatter.

The waka lurches inexplicably, propelled toward the wrecking rock from behind. A log appears from nowhere and rams me again.

"Save yourself, Kai," calls Nani. "The possessed log is mine."

It's too late. There is no way I'll be able to stop Tūātea running into the rock, so I pray. Giant tentacles appear on the rock face, and I feel the waka jar, momentum halted as the opposing force pushes us from the rock.

I'm thrown from my craft and crash with a bone-crunching impact against the rocks.

The world is dark. I cannot feel water, pain, or my body – I'm suspended in nothing. The whispers of the spirit world rustle. I hear sadness, disappointment, and anger. Still, I feel nothing until the vague comforting presence of Tane wraps itself around me, and I wonder if my life in the physical realm ended early, just as Tane's did.

I drift for ages, unsure what I'm supposed to do, paralysed by uncertainty. There are discussions taking place around me, and I think they're about me. One of the voices is familiar and I wonder if Manaia will claim me, but the voice arguing with her is also known to me - Kiriama.

"Release him; it's not his time."

"He came here alone, Manaia, so now his place is with us."

"You are a fool, Kiriama. Kai isn't yours to hold."

"He is my descendant too Manaia, and I am older than you. How dare you presume to tell me what to do."

"The boy has important work to do, Kiriama, and he doesn't have time for your petty schemes."

"Do you think you have the power to stop me, Manaia?"

"I am not the one who overrules you, Kiriama. Are you so blinded by ambition that you don't see who shapes his future?"

Light explodes behind my eyes.

"They cannot have you. You are mine. Go back to your realm and do my work - live."

Tangaroa booms inside my body like an ocean of waves crashing against the reef.

My eyes snap open as the giant squid wraps me in a tentacle and catapults me onto Tūātea. I'm disorientated because I've been gone so long.

With a cough and expulsion of seawater, I'm astounded to find I'm still in the race at the wrecking rock. I seize the paddle and throw myself into steering, sailing us away from danger. Miraculously, I'm no longer injured, so I know Tangaroa intervened to spare me. Sweat runs down my face, and words of thanks spill from my lips as my physical saviour disappears under the waves. My fathers are with me, and Nani turned the log to hinder the competitors behind me.

I must go into the final leg of the race in the lead to have any chance against the raiders' nimble craft. Waves are choppy around me, churned by unseen influences, but the calm Nani created for my waka holds.

Favourable winds power my progress, and the pursuers fall further behind, plagued by random gusts. The reef channel requires different navigating skills, and I'm fortunate to have viewed every bommie, shelf, and rock formation from under the water. Speed is less important here, and I must work with the currents flowing around the many obstacles.

With a flash of inspiration, I clutch the ancestral pounamu Starman entrusted to me for this journey. I feel the power of our tīpuna stir as they navigate from my heart and through my body.

We are one – me, Tūātea, tīpuna, the Gods and the sea. A chant strokes my vocal cords, and a song I never sang before ripples from the core of our melded being. The remainder of the course is like a dream. Ebbing and flowing with the chant, we travel where we will without effort or haste – almost as if the world slows.

My body reacts instinctively, as fluid as the water around me. The joining awakens every vestige of knowledge passed to me as a child. Under the black skies of Walu, the three realms unite, and I'm reborn. They don't assist me merely to win the contest, for this union will wage the war of retribution to come.

Chapter 10

Starman's Son

The blood spirits of Kapanval are no match for my allies. We collect all the tokens without further incident, and I sail past the finishing point well ahead of everyone else.

"That was astonishing, Kai. The older men acknowledge you as Starman's son. Beach your waka, and go to Kapanval," instructs Taka.

His raised eyebrows and bemused look betray his surprise. These men have dominated the region for years, with their seafaring and martial superiority, so losing a contest to an outsider is a novel experience. The fear they inspire in people provides them with an unfair advantage. If I were alone, facing the prospect of being eaten or sacrificed, my confidence and skills may have deserted me.

Stroking Tūātea lovingly, and muttering karakia, I openly give thanks to the Gods who assisted me. My hands move in the flowing gestures I learned from Marama – the spirit language of her home.

People watch me, curious. Kapanval consumed the tohunga, who once communed with the Gods and spirits. Darkness and violence reign on the blood-soaked soil of Walu, and the glimpse of light reminds people of a past they barely remember.

Other competitors finish the race and head for the beach as I make my way to Kapanval.

The chief laughs as I approach his entourage.

"So, Starman's son returns to me. Perhaps you are an even better navigator than he." Kapanval narrows his eyes suspiciously. "Are you also a tohunga," he asks quietly.

"No, I haven't trained or been initiated as a tohunga. My mother's family is deeply spiritual and I'm a son of the sea, so I was raised to honour the Gods."

Every word I utter is the truth, and Kapanval relaxes, safe in the knowledge I'm not a powerful tohunga sent to overthrow him by one of his many enemies.

The rest of the competitors straggle toward us, bemoaning the fickle wind, strange currents, and challenging obstacles. They are hardened men who acknowledge my win and salute my skill, wondering if Kapanval will allow me to join them. Raiding isn't without risk. The sea and weather are more dangerous than most resistance they face, so any opportunity to keep their lives and accumulate wealth is welcomed. Navigators are a fraternity that work together, and they'd like to learn from me.

Kapanval stands and a hush falls over the crowd.

"Kai, son of Starman the navigator, I declare you the winner. Step forward to receive your rewards."

To the sound of raised voices, not exactly cheering, Kapanval hands me the spear, then the club. My world goes black. A cacophony of angry muttering buzzes in my head. Nani comes to my rescue.

"Kai isn't one of them. I am his spirit guide and I place him in danger by communicating with you this way. Foul spirits inhabit this place. Stand down – but know that the Gods and all those who have been wronged seek revenge. We will call you to battle, on the day of reckoning, but you must release the boy now," insists Nani.

I blink, believing I've been somewhere else for a time, but everyone is in the same place, making noise. They look at me expectantly so I raise the weapons over my head, and treat them to a roar, with my tongue protruding - a fierce Maori posture. It elicits a stirring response from the warriors gathered there, who are warming to me. Kapanval looks pleased with himself.

"Tonight, you can claim the last prize when we feast," he laughs. "The women from our last raid will dance to determine their positions on Walu."

My heart sinks, but I muster an enthusiastic smile by imagining the female ancestors punishing Kapanval.

"That's good, Kai. You look feral, which makes you fit in," whispers Nani. "Give them a show, and they will love you."

With a primal scream, I launch into the fiercest haka I know. My chest turns red from the slapping and pounding. Muscles bulge in an impressive display of strength as I pound my feet on the ground, kicking up the sand. Rivulets of sweat stream down my contorted face as the haka comes to a crescendo. I grab my new spear and twirl it like a taiaha. Maui's adopted father Rongo, spent many hours drilling me as a boy until I could parry and thrust in my sleep. At the end of my haka, I jump in the air, land on one knee in front of Kapanval, bow my head, and lay my spear at his feet.

The chief gives me a nod, but that is the extent of his reaction, and he leaves the beach with his entourage in tow. Taka slaps my back, and the navigators raise their paddles in salute. A grinning Pita walks toward me with a fresh coconut to quench my thirst. His excitement tells me he's getting rich by betting on me.

"How much did you win this time, Pita?" I ask between gulps.

He looks around to ensure nobody else is in earshot before replying. "I've made more off you than I did from my last six raids."

I laugh out loud, and people stare at me. Laughter isn't common on Walu.

"Come, Kai. It's only fair I attire you appropriately for the feast tonight and feed you. After all the wealth you've brought me," says Pita with a shrug.

It's my first invitation to eat with anyone since I arrived, which is unusual in the islands, so I trail after

Pita. If I want to rescue Wai in time and assist the tīpuna alliance with their vengeance, I need some freedom of movement.

Pita lives simply, and to my surprise, he's alone. I resist asking questions to satisfy my curiosity because I notice the absence of children and family life on Walu. At first, I assumed it was due to my separation from the village, but now, I don't believe that's the case. Nani might know what's wrong here, and I opt to ask her when she returns.

We dine on mahi mahi grilled over coals and taro with coconut. The food is filling but bland and I acknowledge my mother's tasty cooking has spoiled me. Over lunch, we discuss fishing, my new weapons, and generally neutral topics as we eat.

"Thank you, Pita. Your hospitality is appreciated," I comment, determined to maintain my good manners.

"Long ago, Walu was a welcoming place." He shifts uncomfortably before changing the subject. "I have more garments than I need. So, find something to your liking."

"What is customary to wear to a feast with your chief, Pita? I don't want to offend anyone by turning up looking like a fatherless savage."

Seeking advice from Pita is a good move. He grunts with satisfaction and sorts through the garments carefully.

"Well, if you were my son, I would want you to look respectable and not too showy."

A ghost flits across Pita's face, and I wonder what happened to his son. The expression is gone in a flash, and he grins before holding up his chosen garments.

"The workmanship is fine, and the patterns represent the histories of their origin. It's traditional to wear the best of what we have raided. Appropriately, we've taken these together from other warriors – the spoils of astute gambling. You're a young man with a healthy body, so wear the loin cloth. But, to display your worth, wear the cloak when you arrive. Oil your skin, and bind your hair in the topknot you favour, but no decoration. The shark is sacred to us here. Do you have any teeth?"

"Yes, I have a necklace of mako shark teeth. I caught it when I became a man."

"That's auspicious. Wear it tonight and tell the story of how you acquired the teeth. You could be, and maybe you are, a son of Walu."

I sense Pita wants to say more, but he turns away to repack his hoard.

"Many thanks, Pita. I know I placed you in an unenviable position when I chose you as my second, but I'm sure you agree I made an excellent choice."

"I never imagined it would be such a lucrative arrangement," he guffaws. "It's been a while since I had this much fun at the expense of my own people."

I decide to take a risk. "What was Walu like when you were a boy?"

Pita doesn't respond, and I fear I've made a mistake. He appears to be far away.

"Sun shone brightly nearly every day, and the lagoon was teeming with life. Even the smallest child could feed their family without a waka. But that was a lifetime ago," he says brusquely.

"I'm sorry, Pita, I didn't mean to pry. Eating here with you made me miss my mother." I look away to hide the raw truth of my confession.

"It's ok, boy, but some things are better left in the past."

He escorts me back to my hut, and before he leaves, I spontaneously place my hand on his shoulder.

"In Aotearoa, my home, we hongi – share breath. Do you know the custom?"

"Yes, I've seen it in my travels."

Pita clasps my shoulder, and we share breath. I feel the tendrils of our spirits entwined in greeting with warmth and trust. When Pita opens his eyes wide and searches my face, I know he feels the connection. Neither of us knows what our growing friendship signifies, but I feel less alone here.

Chapter 11

Prizes

As the dull day deepens to shadowy dusk, drumbeats split the air, and Taka arrives to take me to the feast. The scabs on his knuckles remind me how lucky I am, for he's a powerful hulking mass. Torches are lit, and Kapanval is surrounded by women, pandering to his whims. He signals Taka and me to join him.

"Sit – you'll be able to enjoy the entertainment best from here," he commands.

There are several woven mats in front of Kapanval, so we position ourselves where he points. Three other warriors are directed to the mats, and young women bring us food. They are bare-breasted, with downcast eyes, almost invisible as they flit in and out. I hide my pity behind a grimace and fervently hope Nani returns soon. Once everyone has food and drink, Kapanval claps his hands, and the drummers strike up a fast beat.

A parade of girls and women file into the clearing. They look scared, and some of them wear bruises and cuts. Whether the injuries were acquired during their capture or on Walu, I don't know. Kapanval stands, and the drumming stops.

"Tonight, your job is to entertain us with your best dancing. If you please a warrior, he may choose you to cook, clean or share his mat. Should you fail to impress anyone, you will be assigned the most menial tasks and belong to everyone. Your status on Walu is up to you because I don't care if you live or die. If you are difficult, you will be offered as a sacrifice to the blood spirits - so dance well."

The captive's faces freeze in terror. They are herded from the clearing and instructed to come out one at a time by the man in charge. He advises the warriors they can select women at the end of all the dancing - after I choose first.

It appears the women are tokens in a bartering game. My heart sinks but I give a fist pump and whoop of victory. Most of the women are brave. They dance for their lives, utilising every move they've learned in their villages, to the accompaniment of hoots and cheers from the raiders. These men are the elite inner circle of warriors who serve Kapanval, but Taka remains aloof and observant, even here, protecting his chief.

My ignorance of customs gives me an opportunity to seek information.

"When I pick a woman tonight, will I have to provide for her or take her into my home?" I ask.

The man on my left laughs and the ghost of a smile touches Taka's lips.

"No, Kai, you don't have to provide anything. The woman of tonight is for your pleasure alone," says Taka.

"Kapanval provides for the women here, and we are well-cared for, so we can focus on raiding. Food, drink, training, raiding, fighting, competing, and sex is what we live for," says the warrior on the left. Taka leaves to relieve himself, so I strike up a conversation with my neighbour.

"What about your woman and children? Does Kapanval look after them too?"

"Only Kapanval has children here, and he sacrifices his own to the spirits that protect us. The women live in a separate village and do whatever we need them to do," he shrugs. "We have no weakness anymore."

I nod at him in understanding and laugh. The situation here is worse than I thought and not as simple. What I need is Nani's counsel, and I wonder where she is. The dancing progresses, and I concentrate on the proceedings because I must choose a woman.

One of the last dancers is painfully young and reminds me of Aroha. She will be my choice because I want to protect her. I lean forward as she dances, announcing my interest so when I take her, nobody will be surprised. My neighbour slaps me and winks his approval. I beg Papatūānuku and my ancestors' forgiveness for being here.

The last dancer finishes her hula with a flourish, and men call out, showering her with lewd remarks and gestures. A smile is pasted on the dancer's stony face, and she doesn't flinch, although the behaviour of the crowd is deteriorating. The dancers parade into the fire and torchlight so we can see them. Kapanval stands to address his men.

"A fine catch!" The men cheer their leader enthusiastically. "You will enjoy the fruit of your raid tonight," laughs Kapanval, baring his blackened teeth. "But, the first choice was won by Kai. Victorious warrior, take your pick."

"You honour me, Kapanval. Thank you, esteemed warriors, for harvesting these sweet fruits from the sea. The choice is difficult because I imagine how well they would all hula on my mat." My joke is appreciated with whistles. "I prefer fruit before it gets too ripe, so I choose that one." I point to the young girl, and my neighbour slaps my back with a nod.

"No! Take me instead," begs the last dancer.

"What is a man to do? I know I'm handsome, but I only won one of you," I joke. The men applaud my banter.

"Please, please, pick me. I will give you a night of passion you won't forget." She raises smouldering eyes to meet mine, and I notice the resemblance between her and the girl.

"You are beautiful. Certainly, an energetic dance partner and I would love to take you both," I say, swivelling my hips in a dance display to more laughing, "but Kapanval grants me only one choice."

"Let him have them both," calls my neighbour clapping. Men hoot and call out my name, and the drumbeats start, so I carry on with my dance. I make it comical, acting out a night trying to satisfy two women with gestures and expressive faces. At home, we do impromptu skits to amuse ourselves, and I'm good at it. When I finish, everyone is crying with laughter – even Kapanval.

"You can have them both," shouts Kapanval. "Taka, they can 'sleep' in the guest hut tonight," he says, drying tears of laughter. "Be careful that one doesn't kill you in your sleep," he gestures to the last dancer with a grimace.

"She'll be so tired she won't be able to walk or lift a hand against me. My thanks for your generosity," I say, hand on my chest to show deference and respect.

"You are one of us, Kai – welcome," announces Kapanval.

The men turn their attention to the dancers, and competition commences. Taka and a guard prod my women, and we set off for our hut; I fall back to walk with Taka.

"How does this work? Do they stay with me the whole night, or can I get rid of them or go home once I'm done? I don't plan on letting her kill me," I grin.

"You are smarter than you look," Taka grunts. "In her village," he points to the last dancer, "she wore rank. The girl is her daughter. When you are finished, return to your hut, it's safer. Tie the mother up tightly if you intend to have fun with the girl."

"Perhaps my greed wasn't such a great idea," I sigh.

"You are one lucky bastard," snorts Taka.

Chapter 12

Escape

Girl and woman huddle together, hands bound. If Kapanval baited a trap for me, I'm in trouble but the woman's plea seemed spontaneous so I took the risk.

"I'm not going to hurt you, but when I slap my thigh, I want one of you to scream."

They look at each other and when I slap my leg, the girl squeals.

"We need to make noises like we're struggling."

Eyes wide, they follow my lead, moving around thumping the screens, and making sounds of exerting themselves. I slap my thigh again and this time the mother curses loudly, hurling abuse at me.

"If you behave badly, you miss out Mama and you can spend the whole night tied up," I shout.

"No! I promised you passion. Take me, it's me you want," Mama shouts back. Her daughter watches our play-acting, scared but attentive.

"Passion," I whisper.

The mother starts moaning. She grabs me and starts bumping her hips rhythmically against the wall. I pant and groan as if I'm making love - fast and furious. The girl covers her mouth with a hand to stifle laughter, and I can't resist rolling my eyes to make it harder. Mama and I speed up, slow down, then speed up again with the bumping and moans because I'm sure the guard will eavesdrop. He won't get a woman and I have two. Finally, we reach a noisy crescendo and can take a rest.

Holding my finger to my lips for quiet, I pull them both close and whisper, "I'm not from here. We have to escape. This is our only chance." They nod in eager agreement. "We must keep up the act because the later it is, the more people sleep. What are your names?"

"I'm Savani and this is my daughter Isa," she whispers back.

"Right my pretty pearl. I hope you're as good as your mother," I bellow.

"No, Kai, take me again. I want you," pleads Savani.

Our charade of passion is surprisingly exhausting but we carry on. I leave the hut to relieve myself and do some snooping. There are the usual sounds of a village at night after a feast. People snoring, but no huts as noisy as ours and no guards in sight. As Taka told me to return to my hut, I have a reason to walk around. I return to the hut to brief the girls. They weren't in my escape plan but I can't leave them, my mother was once taken by other people.

"Make two mounds of sand to look like your bodies. I will return to my hut, and you must follow me. Be quiet and alert. There are guards and people moving about the village, try to avoid them. If you're caught, tell them I promised you more sex but when you woke up I was gone. Ask them if they know where I sleep and tell them you want to please Kapanval by keeping your promise to me." I have them repeat the story because it's likely they will be caught and they must be believable. "Don't come to the hut if you aren't caught. My waka Tūātea is on the beach. It's larger than the other vessels and has a whale's tail carved on the back. Wait in the shadow of the waka. The tide will be high soon, and we must get to the water."

Humming to myself, I exit the hut and meander toward the beach. I know the women follow me, but they're stealthy. I plan to greet the guard, but he's sleeping soundly. My karakia is brief but laden with thanks and supplications.

Somewhere the moon is bright but here the dark clouds are my friends, obscuring my shape as I creep toward my waka.

"An interesting night, Kai," says Nani.

I'm relieved she's returned. Getting the waka in the water and past the reef without being seen poses a challenge.

"Tell me about it, Nani. I missed you, but your timing is impeccable. We need to get out of here. Kapanval gifted me a woman for winning a race, I ended up with two, and we have to take them with us. It's a long story."

"Clearly, I'm not the only one having adventures to-night," chuckles Nani.

"It's dark here Nan, but can you help hide us while we launch and navigate the reef?"

"I must be careful not to alert those bloody spirits, but yes, I can shield you for a short time."

To my surprise, Savani and Isa make it to Tūātea without being challenged. Most of my gear is stowed aboard and the rest is packed, for a swift departure.

"Night is darkening for you Kai, go swiftly and may the Gods guide you," murmurs Nani.

Her blessing is welcome, but the encouragement to hurry is unnecessary as I'm possessed by a sense of urgency to leave Walu in my wake.

Crouching low in thick gloom, I run on silent feet to my waka. It's so dark I startle a sharp breath from Isa when she feels me beside her. Feeling for their faces I place two fingers over their lips and pull them close behind me so they can feel my movement.

If they help me push the waka to the water it will be quicker, but not all cultures allow women to partici-pate in launching waka. Fortunately, the woman and girl lend their muscles to my efforts and we slide toward the water's edge as silently as possible.

Tāwhirimātea covers our tracks, the moon hides her light, Nani's darkness holds and Tangaroa reaches fin-gers for my waka. I heave the girl, then the woman aboard Tūātea before propelling the craft into deeper water and clambering on. The water sucks us rapidly to the reef channel and as I set sail the wind fills it. Eager Gods whisk us away as angry blood spirits begin to stir with a mournful howl.

Figures run onto the beach and congregate where Tūātea lay. They are barely discernable in the gloom, but raised voices send snatches of shouting over the water. All eyes are trained on the water but they are unable to see us. I focus on navigating us through the reefs and channels, merging with the ocean and my sea father.

Unnatural light bursts in the sky and the spirit screams batter our ears with a discordant cacophony. The men on the shore spot us and the chase begins. We are almost in the open water and I feel the triumphant surge in the waves and wind.

"Well done little brother," Ira encourages me.

"Flee, Kai. Use all your skill. Sail where the wind and ocean take you," sighs Nani.

My passengers huddle together and I position them for safety and balance. When the Gods, your whale brother, and spirit guide tell you to run – you run for your life.

Never before have I sailed at such speed. With the current pulling me and the wind pushing me in the same direction, the waka is flying. There are moments when I'm unsure if the waka and the sea are connected because we leap from wave crest to wave crest. Tūātea is exultant; it's as if his namesakes steer. I cannot keep the joy from my face, and I call greetings to my coconspirators as a waiata rolls off my tongue. It's not a song I've sung before but it lives in me - a song of the sons of the sea, rolling forth like thunderous breakers on rocks.

The happiness of practising my sea-craft makes me forget I have passengers. They probably think I'm mad.

"I'm sorry for my neglect and ill-manners wāhine, but we must put distance between us and Walu," I shout.

"The Gods are on your side Kai and we are content with the growing distance," calls Savani.

"I've never been so fast," squeals Isa. She isn't afraid, just exhilarated.

If the pursuing waka made it past the lagoon, we never saw them. We race our way to freedom.

Chapter 13

Vengeance

Once we are safe at sea, I drop anchor and tell my passengers, I must try and save the other women. Ira is there to watch over them, but there's no time to explain our relationship.

Nani comes to my rescue and sings them to sleep so I lay down to join her in the spirit world for battle. I feel the turbulence of the void.

"Come, Kai, it's time to end this feud. Your tīpuna are here and we rid the world of Kapanval, his raiders, and their evil with the blessing of the Gods."

"Nani, there are many innocent women and children in a separate village on the other side of Walu from Kapanval. Starman's sister and some cousins. Can we save them?"

"You made a spiritual connection to the man, Pita. He was abducted as a boy like Starman. If we hurry, we can

use him to save them or at least try but we are angry in this realm."

"I can feel it, Nani. Please tell me what to do?"

The presence of Tane calms me and we prepare for the coming battle together.

Taka reports my escape to Kapanval and he unleashes his fury on the men. They cluster on the beach attempting to launch waka to pursue me but the waves are enormous. It's impossible to launch and the fierce wind scours their skin with sand.

Kapanval grabs one of his men and slits his throat, to offer his leaking life to the blood spirits, so they will pursue me. The rising shriek of the swarming blood spirits scares the bravest of men but Kapanval exults in their bloodlust. All his will and efforts are focused on punishing me, an advantageous situation for my tīpuna.

While the evil spirits are feasting, I find Pita cleaning his nails in the guard house. Wisely, he's keeping a low profile due to his association with me but sent his men to participate in the launching fiasco. I hover above him, not sure what to do next.

One of Pita's tipuna comes to assist me - his grandmother. She flows through the connection I've made with Pita, to deliver him a message.

"Pita, these are not our people. I am your grandmother. They stole you from us and we are here to avenge our dead. Go quickly to the women, launch the foraging vessels and we will save them, and you. Everyone on the Black Island will perish."

The blood drains from Pita's face, and he shakes his head as if to dislodge the voice. He's still for a few moments. Pita grabs his weapons, checks nobody is around, and runs straight to the Women's Village. Arriving short of breath, he goes straight to the guard hut and demands they wake their leader. The leader knows Pita, they are of equal rank and respect one another.

"Gather your men. Kapanval summons us all. That stranger, Kai, who won the race has escaped with two of our women. I've sent all my men to the beach with Taka and he asked me to stay here so you can join him with your guards. Perhaps he blames me for losing the throwing contest," Pita complains.

The other leader nods his assent and sympathy at Pita. I admire Pita's quick thinking and Nani chuckles her approval. Pita doesn't waste time. He frees the prisoners and tells them to launch the waka before rousing those sleeping, and telling them to flee for their lives. The women are shocked but most have dreamed of escape since they arrived, so don't hesitate. There's no time to search for my relatives but I see a vessel streaking ahead and I know it's my aunt because she paddles like Starman and the current carries them to safety.

As the innocent captives escape, Nani and I join the other spirits for the battle. We hover over the island, watching people the size of insects and hideous blood spirits, bloated on Kapanval's slain guard. From a spiritual perspective, Kapanval is a dense black shadow rather than a man. The writhing souls of the people he's eaten are trapped in his evil wairua - a fate worse than death.

The flaming taiaha of Tane appears at my side, and he hands me his mere, which pulses with its own spirit. Poised for the strike, the hoard descends releasing the pent-up fury of ages. Blood spirits shriek and Kapanval looks up. He summons his ancestors to meet us as we hoped he would.

The spirits clash with a blast that flattens everything on Walu. Men are stunned and confused before they're cut down by avenging wraiths. The battle rages, and the howls of vanquished blood spirits pollute the air. Fighting is furious, and Tane, Nani, and I move together, weapons hissing as we engage our foes.

There are too many of us, and we overwhelm the evil spirits. Kapanval stands isolated before us in the spirit world, his body slumped in the physical realm. He gained access to the realm through a tohunga he lured to Walu.

Tane strikes the blow to sever Kapanval's ties and banish him to the physical world where his body is ageing rapidly and wracked with intense pain. Our work is almost done, although a few wily blood spirits escape and must be hunted down. The offended Gods will strike the final blow, and we retreat for safety.

A twisting spiral of cyclonic wind sucks up huts, trees, and people, laying waste to the Black Island as Tāwhirimātea roars his displeasure and takes Kapanval to enjoy a slow and painful death.

To assuage his annoyance, Tangaroa cleanses the islands under massive waves, removing any trace of the raiders' existence. He sends his creatures to inhabit the waters with the giant squid and takes any fouled ones to repair.

When the Gods have taken their vengeance, the Black Island - Walu, is no more. In its place are pristine uninhabited islands that await the gifts of other Gods.

The clash was brutal but we are triumphant and the satisfied murmuring of the spirit hoard is deafening. Manaia, Nani, and Tane surround me with our own korero, and I feel I belong here.

"One day, my son, you'll join us. You're right; you do have a place here with us. But Tangaroa gave you a quest that will endure through time and continue through your descendants, so you must return. You also have Marama, Starman, and your siblings to return to one day," Tane reminds me.

"And don't forget, Kai, that you have me as your guide," says Nani.

She senses my reluctance to leave and Nani has experienced this issue with my mother. I know they are right, and I must return to my body. Leaving Tane, my father isn't easy - especially after being in battle together.

With a sigh, I am back in my physical body, breathing air and lulled by the steady beating heart.

Chapter 14

Wai

Rā (the sun) paints the horizon in soft pinks and purples. I greet the light with morning karakia and praise the night for guarding my waka. The spiritual battle didn't last long in physical time. In the glorious sunrise, Kali leaps into the air, chittering a friendly greeting and rousing Isa, from sleep.

"Look, Mama! It's a dolphin."

"Her name is Kali. She and Wai are companions, and Kali's happy to see us because she's worried," I frown. "When you can't speak to your kaitiaki, it means one of you is in trouble."

"Come, Isa, we must sit out of the way and let Kai sail."

"Thanks, Savani, and can you pass me a dried kumara? I'm hungry."

"I bet you're always hungry," giggles Isa, earning a sharp look from her mother.

My heart lurches because Aroha always teases me about my bottomless puku.

An island specks on the horizon, and Ira reassures me it's where I'll find Wai. The dolphin's concern is contagious, and I empathise with her anxiety, goading me to push Tūātea to a racing pace. Ira creates a slipstream with his wake. The shore beckons, palm trees waving me to hurry, so I drop anchor in the bay and body surf to the beach. I'm tired, but my sense of urgency fuels my limbs.

"Please let me be in time," I mumble.

The camp is devoid of guards, but their belongings are scattered randomly. I wonder what happened to them because there is no life here but Wai. I shudder as I pick up a water gourd. It's only a short distance to the cave, but I arrive winded after the run.

The silence is eerie. Wai is here, and I must locate her quickly, so I allow my eyes to adjust to the gloom. There are footprints all over the sand inside the cave and a cooking fire, mat, garments, and a comb but no sign of Wai.

She hid so well that the guards never expected to find her in the cave. The flaw in the plan was that guards remained there in case she returned, preventing her escape to the beach.

I weigh the rocks with my eyes. Wai could've moved rocks at full strength but maybe couldn't budge them after a couple of days. When I try to move the rocks, most are too heavy or too light.

Closing my eyes, I try and connect with her wairua – imploring her heartbeat to speak to me. My eyes flick upward. Clever Wai climbed the cavern wall and found a boulder niche. It's the size I'm looking for, and I detect a fading life force. I climb the wall and heave the stone out of the way. It's heavy, and I'm unsure how Wai pulled it inward so tightly – perhaps the strength of desperation because she is curled behind it.

There isn't much space to manoeuvre, so I wet her lips. When they part, I dribble one drop at a time into her mouth. Wai is the girl in my dream. Gaunt now, but as achingly beautiful as I remember.

Tears well in my eyes, and I blink and swallow to stop them falling – I don't have time to feel emotional. The memory of chubby, gap-toothed painful Wai as a child makes me smile. I clean her face and continue to administer the water. I can't move her until I can strap her to my body.

Climbing down carefully, I light the fire, return to the camp and find food to make broth. The guards have ample supplies, and I help myself to fibrous rope and garments to secure Wai for the descent. She is slight, her curves melted, fretting about Kali, and Wai is easy to carry, even though she's unconscious. Once I fasten Wai to my back, I climb down.

The fire radiates heat, and I gently lower Wai onto a pile of mats and cover her to keep her warm. I need to beach Tūātea, get my healing supplies, and organise nutritious food for Wai. For a moment, I forgot about

Savani and Isa, but they must come ashore and make camp. Taking care of Wai may be a good distraction for them.

"Ira, I'm returning. Tell Kali Wai lives, but she needs care. Wai is unconscious, so Kali has no idea how she is. I know how horrible that feels from when I lost you."

"I'll tell her, and I'm touched our separation affected you so deeply."

I feel his sincerity and smile, and I wonder how we coped with parting each year. Now we are close so much of the time; we're an extension of each other. The swim to the waka is invigorating, and I spot juicy crustaceans on the way. Streaming water, my head pops over the side of the boat.

"Did you find her?" Isa squeals wringing her hands.

I didn't consider Savani and Isa worrying about Wai. It's stupid of me because it's the way of women to care for one another - one of many gifts from Papatūānuku.

"Yes, I found her. She's unconscious. We'll beach the waka and make camp until she revives. I'm sorry to delay your return home, but I can't move Wai in her current state."

"No need to apologise, Kai. We're grateful you took us from Walu and we hope Isa and I can help look after Wai until her health returns."

Savani and Isa are good people, always helpful, and I'm happy to have company.

"I did see some delicious prawns on the swim back. Do you know how to catch them?" I ask.

"You are looking at the best prawn and crab catcher in our village," boasts Isa.

Grabbing one of my nets, she jumps overboard.

"I'll meet you at the camp," she yells.

"She's full of life, my Isa," laughs Savani. "And she's a great provider, so we'll never be hungry between the two of you."

"My mother would love her, Savani because she's exactly the same."

Savani and I quickly unload supplies when we land, and she makes camp while I tend to Wai. There is fresh water to be fetched, sleeping places to organise, and coconuts to be gathered and husked. The help leaves me free to focus on Wai.

Growing up with Marama, I've absorbed some of her healing skills and start a thorough diagnosis. Wai is suffering from dehydration and perhaps starvation, but I can't find any other ailments. Her wairua is weak, and a shadow stains it, maybe grief over losing Kali.

"Will she live, Kai?" asks Savani.

"I hope so. Come in, Savani. I want to offer karakia to the Earth Mother and ask for assistance to heal Wai. It could be helpful if you join me."

Savani kneels on the opposite side of Wai, we join hands, and I let Marama flow through me. Her prayers, heard so often as a child, tumble from my lips. When I open my eyes, Savani stares at me with brimming tears.

"That was wonderful, Kai. I'm moved by your invocation to Earth Mother. Where did you learn that?"

"My mother is a healer and spirit guide, descended from a long line of exceptional women. She's the keeper of our ancestral knowledge until my sister takes her place."

"I believe Wai has more colour in her cheeks, Kai. Shall we try a few drops of broth?"

"Good idea, Savani. We must restore her strength. When she reconnects with Kali, the healing will be faster. I have a rub for her limbs to aid blood flow and warm her."

"Would you like me to do that for you? If she's an unpartnered woman, having a mother tend to her needs might be more acceptable. I can also bathe and dress her."

"Thanks, Savani, that would be great. If you take care of Wai, I'll help Isa and cook us a feast."

"You must be tired, Kai. Last night you hardly slept. Please rest, and Isa and I will prepare food. It's the least we can do for you."

I realise Savani is right. For the last two nights, I've sailed without rest. As soon I lie on a mat, sleep claims me.

Hunger wakes me. I've slept the whole day, and my stomach rumbles a complaint. The tantalising smell of prawns cooking on the fire prises my droopy eyelids apart.

"Come on, Kai, I've cooked you the best prawns on the coals," grins Isa.

"How is Wai?"

"She's resting comfortably and taking small amounts of water and broth the whole day. Wai is washed, dressed, and I've rubbed her limbs as you instructed," said Savani.

"You were right. I needed sleep, and now I'm starving. Hand them over, Isa."

The prawns are succulent, lightly charred, and served with coconut, fresh seaweed, and reef fish. I eat everything Isa puts in front of me, wash it down with coconut water, lick my fingers, and she beams her satisfaction. Savani smiles and gives Isa a nod of appreciation.

I wash my hands and go to check Wai. She's still pale, face pinched in pain at times. Her body requires sustenance but must become accustomed to food again.

"Ira, we need Nani. I feel I'm missing something because Wai should be improving. Can we reach for her together?"

We seek Nani together.

"I'm here, Kai," says Nani faintly.

"Nani, I'm no healer, but I grew up with Marama, and Wai isn't responding as she should. A lack of food and water I can easily remedy. There's a faint shadow on her wairua. Could that be the cause of her illness?"

"Your instincts are good, mokopuna. We're hunting blood spirits, and one of them may be hiding in Wai. They are foul and pollute their host. If you can extract it, Kai, I can destroy it."

"How can I get it out, Nani?" I swallow because I'm unfamiliar with the task.

"You step into the spiritual realm and summon it with blood into the physical. I know you haven't experienced being guided, but I'll be with you. Prepare yourself with karakia, and cleanse your body. Send the women to the outside camp where they'll be safe. Tell them not to return to the cave if they hear screaming because those spirits are howlers."

"I'll be here too, little brother, anchoring you in the physical world," Ira reassures me. He senses how nervous I am.

Savani looks alarmed when I give the instructions to her and Isa but nods sternly in agreement.

"Kai, I cleanse our spiritual leader for ceremonies in my village. May I prepare you for this – task?"

"Thank you, Savani."

Far away from Aotearoa and my family, I believe it's wise to have the support of local people. There is a wholesomeness and positivity about Savani and Isa that may help counteract the blood spirit.

I submit to the ministrations of Savani, and she moves through her karakia of cleansing and preparation. She anoints my body with oil before kneeling and inclining her head. Her spirituality shines around her, and her efforts move me.

"My thanks, Savani. Your support fortifies me for the battle ahead."

There is nothing left to do but tackle the blood spirit. The thought makes me shiver, but I'm ready, and Nani and Tane will be with me. One look at Wai encourages me to hurry. She is pale again, and her breath is shallow. Taking her hand in mine, I close my eyes and clear my mind.

The world is black. Marama has described the void of the next realm to me, I've been in a spirit battle, so I don't panic. I wait for what feels like an eternity before I hear a sigh and whispering.

"Well, what do we have here?" asks a voice old as crumbling stone.

It's her again, a spirit I wasn't expecting. Grateful for my mother's lessons, I know to be polite, not to ask the spirit's name, and to be cautious. The spirit has diverted Nani and Tane to find me first – not good. I'm a novice in this realm.

"Greetings, illustrious spirit. I am but a humble boy awaiting the arrival of his Kuia. Thank you for speaking to such an unimportant person. Are you my tipuna?"

"Yes, our bloodlines have crossed. Welcome, dear boy. Perhaps I am meant to be your spirit guide?"

In a flash of inspiration, I remember my mother's story of her encounter with the spirit Kiriama. I believe it's her because Manaia argued with her, and she knows who I am.

"Can it really be you, ancestral mother? My mother, grandmother, and spirit guide have spoken of you."

"Your whanau have long memories, boy," she remarks, sounding displeased.

So, I identify Kiriama correctly, which means I'm in danger. I need to stall until Nani and Tane locate me.

"Why wouldn't we remember you, ancestral mother? You were the first spirit my mother encountered in this realm, and she talks about you still. She was such a young girl and never dreamed a spirit of your longevity would be interested in her." I prattle on lavishing as much praise on Kiriama as I can. *"And now, you have granted me an audience as well. I can't wait to tell her!"*

"Do you think she will be pleased that I have found you and will be your spirit guide?"

"A good point, ancient one. Actually, I believe my mother will be as jealous as an eel in a hinaki (eel trap) watching me swim downstream," I chuckle.

"You have a sense of humour as well. I believe we are made for each other, and our alliance will make an impact across the realms, dear boy. What is your name?"

"My name is Kai, and I am pleased to make your acquaintance."

Kiriama hasn't asked me to accept her as my spirit guide yet, but she will. Then I'll have to reject her, exposing myself to her anger in the spiritual realm. I need to keep her engaged. *"I'm not entirely sure how Kai came to be my name. It isn't the name of my physical father or my spirit father, Tane."* I hope by saying Tane, I will call him to me. *"Even my sea father isn't named Kai, but there is only one Tangaroa."*

"You are a son of the sea?"

"Yes. Do you know my sea father?"

There's no answer. Kiriama is gone, leaving me alone in the void again. Whispers surround me. Gentle at first, but becoming louder.

"*Kai, we are here,*" murmurs Nani.

"*Nani, thank goodness. Tane, I mean father, did you hear me?*"

"*Yes, I did. That was smart thinking, son, to name us both. That evil spirit sent us both sailing on a false tide, then wrapped you so we couldn't find you. Lucky Marama shared her stories with you.*"

"*We are running out of time, Nani. What do I need to do?*" I beg.

"*Tane and I will take you to the edge of the void. You need to reach into Wai with your spiritual self, using the proximity of your body. Offer the spirit blood. It will be thirsty because Kapanval fed them well, and it is draining Wai. Ask your physical self to offer blood as you would to Tangaroa. It is difficult to compel your body with your spirit at first, but I will help you. When the blood spirit emerges, I can expel it from here and send it where it belongs. Tane will guard the entrance to the spiritual realm to prevent it from finding a protector. Repeat the instructions back to me.*"

I'm used to repeating instructions because Marama made me do it my whole life. When Nani is satisfied I know what to do; we perch on the precipice between the realms. My hand clasps Wai, and I flow into her form with a push from Nani. The shadow is there in her wairua, but now I can see its shape.

"Blood spirit, this is no place for you in this weak, dying body. I offer you blood as a reward. You must be thirsty."

"She has lots of blood, fool," it sneers.

"And when she dies? You trap yourself in a carcass with no master to serve. Kapanval is destroyed, and you need someone to feed you, stupid one. There are many floating spirits like you, and other men don't have blood like mine. Are you such an idiot that you don't recognise me for what I am?" I opt to mimic its insulting behaviour.

It regards me with distrust, but its greed betrays the spirit. I see the bloodlust in red eyes, and a lizard tongue licks its lips.

It's time to draw blood, so I focus on moving my hand to my knife. Nothing moves, although I concentrate hard. Nani is with me, so I try again, and my effort rewards me with a twitch. Then with a surge of energy, my hand lurches, grasps the knife, and pierces my leg. A trickle of blood runs down my thigh.

The spirit makes a dash. It's quick and fastens itself to my thigh before I comprehend where it is. Nani jumps from her merge with me to seize the blood spirit, but it slithers from her grasp, mouth smeared with my blood. The spirit is desperate because it knows Nani can destroy it. It runs up the cave wall with Nani in pursuit, then dives from the roof – into my vacant body.

Chapter 15

Complications

We did not plan this. I'm now physically possessed by the blood spirit. Nani can't destroy the blood spirit while it's inside me, or I'll be damaged. Instinctively, I return to my body. The blood spirit is jubilant because my body is extraordinarily healthy, and I despair because it won't want to leave. I doubt it can understand whale communication, so I consult Nani and Ira.

"Now, what do I do? That foul creature is polluting my insides. Do you believe I can expand my spirit and squeeze it out?"

"Not a bad idea, Kai. But, I believe it will soon leave your body," says Ira.

"Ira is right. You are a son of the sea, and salt runs in your veins. It will feed greedily and develop an unquenchable thirst - torture," says Nani. "While we wait you can take Wai to the women. They'll tend her, and she will recover. Return to the cave immediately because we must catch that slippery worm when it emerges. I'm tired and too slow, so I've asked Tane to help me. My grandmother, Manaia, will guard the next realm."

I feel strange with the spirit residing inside me, but scooping Wai into my arms, I follow the instructions. Savani and Isa are relieved to see me and notice Wai is no longer pale.

"What's wrong, Kai? Are you sick?" asks Savani.

"I still have work to do, Savani, and I must return to the cave. When you hear the howling, don't worry, it means my task is complete."

Her firm brown hand squeezes Isa's shoulder, stopping the questions she wants to ask.

The blood spirit taunts me with its thirst, but I refuse to drink. It incites nausea and a rebellion in my stomach that makes me vomit. However, I'm in peak condition, so I meditate and repay the spirit with repulsive visions – aroha, whanau, laughter, and my guiding spirits. Ira plunges me into the ocean, and he swims and cavorts for the joy of living.

During my karakia to Tangaroa, expressing my love and devotion, the spirit can stand me no longer. It separates in a desperate rush from my repugnant body with a demonic howl and scoots upwards, but Tane anticipates the trajectory of the spirit and spins his flaming taiaha. Nani cackles from the cavemouth, her ember bowl awaiting breath, and traps the blood spirit. I clasp my mere, ready to strike if it tries to enter my body.

My body is the only safe place for the spirit, and it leaps from the wall toward my head. But Tane is too quick. The screams are hideous as the taiaha cuts a flaming arc through its tormented body, banishing it from the realm of the living. All that remains are the shrieking echoes bouncing from stone to stone.

Nani, Tane and I celebrate our victory with karakia. It's another battle we've won against evil spirits, and we work well together. Spending time with my spirit father and Nani is a dream come true, so I feel buoyant. As our ritual of thanks finishes, Nani reminds me of my earthly duties.

"Go to the women and Wai, Kai. They are worried and need to know you have won."

I know Nani is correct, but I linger a moment, reluctant to be parted again from Tane. He salutes me and fades back into his realm, leaving me with a better understanding of my mother.

"Thanks, Nan. I'll bring Wai back to good health."

The white faces and crinkled brows that greet me speak volumes – the screaming scared Savani and Isa. Happily, Wai is still unconscious, so she has no idea what transpired.

"Kai!"

Isa runs to me and throws her arms around my middle, wiping her tears on my chest.

"Oh, Isa! I'm so sorry the blood spirit scared you."

"Are you ok?" she sobs.

"Yes, I'm ecstatic to be rid of that monster. And I'm starving," I mutter.

"Get Kai some food Isa and some coconut juice. He's won a battle and needs replenishing. Come, hurry," she urges.

Savani knows giving Isa something useful to do will dissipate her shock, and she hugs me with a grin.

"I thought there was something amiss, Kai. It entered your body?"

"Yes, it did. Nasty little creature made me feel quite sick, and now I want to eat a school of fish with every coconut on the island."

The laughter makes us feel better, and my two rescued women watch me eat huddled together. Once I've dealt with my hunger, I check on Wai.

"How is she, Savani?"

"Breathing is more regular, and her body is warm. We massaged her limbs and dribbled water and broth into her mouth."

After I've cleansed myself, I examine Wai. My mother's voice plays in my head, coaching me through the healing ritual of checking health – body, mind, and spirit. As I clasp her hand, Ira arrives with Kali, who infuses Wai with her vitality and strength. When I open my eyes, Wai is flushed, blood suffusing her face, and a smile of contentment lights her features.

Wai is lovely, and her vulnerability touches me, so I think perhaps I'm too hard on her. We are no longer children engaging in petty squabbles. Her horrible tricks are in the past, and my role is to protect and take her home.

Ira is near, so I swim out to him as the void left by Tane creates a sense of loss. I realise how lucky my mother was to find love again because there's something magnetic about my spirit father's presence. Marama told me frankly of her battle with the desire to die so she could be with him. I didn't understand at the time, but now I empathise.

"Ah! The bond between you and Tane has grown, little brother. Was ever a calf so lucky."

"What do you mean, Ira? I feel lost whenever he leaves me."

"Sometimes you can be slow, Kai. You have fathers who love and treasure you in three realms. Starman, Tane, and Tangaroa are all outstanding in their own right. Most boys are grateful to have one good father, and the Gods bless you with a trio. And you have outstanding siblings," quips Ira with a splash of his tail.

"Yes, I do. Aroha and Maui are certainly gifted," I laugh, excluding Ira on purpose.

Ira tosses me in the air, so I plummet headfirst into the sea. My reward for being cheeky. Kali joins us in our play, buoyed by the prospect of Wai regaining her health and reuniting with her. The time flies, and when I return to the island to show her gratitude, Kali herds reef fish toward the shore making fishing easy. I rapidly spear a generous catch.

Savani and Isa aren't idle. The smell of baking coconut cakes flavoured with flower nectar greets me, along with smoking fish and seaweed soup. I check on Wai, and she sleeps soundly. We gut the fresh fish, singing companionably while we work, content with our freedom and abundance of kai. Savani adds fish to her soup and some seawater for seasoning, and Isa shyly brings me a coconut cake wrapped in leaves to sample.

"Isa, this is delicious. As good as my mother's. But, if you ever meet Marama, don't tell her I said that. She's extremely proud of her cooking," I grin.

"I would like to meet your mother. Can you take us home to visit one day?" asks Isa.

Her eyes are wide and hopeful. I'm surprised the lure of another adventure tempts her already; she isn't even home from her first ordeal. Isa is an extraordinary girl.

"Come now, Isa, we still have to find our way home," laughs Savani, shaking her head.

There's a glint of pride in Savani's eyes even though she scolds Isa, and I suspect they have loved ones pining for them somewhere. I hope Wai will recover swiftly.

I spend the rest of the day attending to the waka, mending my gear, and stowing supplies. Finally, my grumbling stomach can no longer resist the aroma of food. We dedicate time to intricate karakia before indulging in a long and hearty meal.

We try and outdo each other by telling our most entertaining stories, singing enthusiastically, and dancing. The noise stirs Wai.

Tentatively, she raises herself on shaky elbows. I rush over to her, overwhelmed by a sense of relief from Kali received via Ira. Wai stares at me, eyes wide with disbelief. Tears mist my eyes, and I gently put my hand on hers.

"You're free, Wai. It's Kai, and I've come to reunite you with Kali and take you home."

She slumps against me with a gentle sob, and I realise the rebonding with Kali is intense. After losing Ira, I understand what's happening.

"Please, Wai. While you are awake, take some water and broth. The time trapped in the cave has depleted your body, and we must restore your strength before we can travel."

Wai nods her head gently and allows me to feed her sips of water and soup before closing her eyes again.

"Did she speak to you, Kai?" asks Savani.

"Not yet, but I talked to her, and she understood me. I'm encouraged that she's taken water and soup. We'll voyage as soon as she's well enough to travel. Thank you both for a wonderful evening and meal. Let's get some rest in the arms of Papatūānuku while we can."

My paddle arm is twitchy the next day. The waves whisper on the sand, 'come and sail with us.' The moon is waxing, and the stars wheeling overhead pull at me, so I know the time to leave is near. Wai has improved markedly. She sits up with a jerk, wiping the sleep from her eyes.

"Easy, Wai. You're ok but still weak," I caution.

Isa and Savani are making food at the cooking fire.

"Who are they?" asks Wai.

"A woman and her daughter I rescued from Kapanval on Walu."

"I stalled my match-making for a whole cycle of the stars, waiting for you to arrive. Then you finally show up, late, to rescue me - with two other women in tow!"

Her voice is shrill, mildly hysterical even. I remain calm and silent because that's what Marama would do with a recovering patient.

"Don't you have anything to say for yourself?" she spits at me.

Her eyes are a storm of anger, and I squirm uncomfortably under their gaze. The reaction isn't what I was expecting. For the past few days, we've been fighting for her life, and I never imagined she would be angry with me.

"Calm yourself, Wai. A blood spirit possessed your body, and you lost much of your strength. Kali awaits your recovery, as do we, so we can leave this island," I reply gently.

A hurled coconut bowl ricochets off my shoulder, and Wai lies back down on the mat with her hands over her eyes breathing erratically. I'm unsure what to do but don't want to upset her further, so I return to my companions.

"Kai, I saw Wai sit up. How is she?" Savani asks, excitement lighting her face.

"Recovering, I think. But Wai is furious with me. I'm going to spend some time with Ira and give Wai some healing space," I mumble.

Savani frowns and looks confused but inclines her head graciously.

I'm confused. Wai was expecting me to arrive and save her, but finding her wasn't a simple task. The sea beckons and I dive in, eager to be in my element.

"Troubled, little brother?"

"Ae (yes), Ira. Wai is as complicated as ever. We voyage all the way from Aotearoa, get side-tracked from my task for Tangaroa, and I risk my life by going to Walu to look for her – and she's mad at me for taking so long." Now I sound hysterical. "I just don't understand her. And how am I supposed to get her in condition to travel when she's an emotional wreck?"

My body tingles with Ira's amusement which irritates me. "You aren't helping."

"Sorry, Kai, but I find your predicament entertaining – forgive me?"

"I'll think about it," I reply huffily.

"What exactly did Wai say?"

"That she's been expecting me for a cycle of seasons, that I'm late, and she's annoyed that I rescued Savani and Isa before her."

"Ah."

"What do you mean – ah! Is there some great secret nobody is sharing with me?"

"There's no need to take your mood out on me, Kai. I perceive the problem, and clearly, you do not. If you don't want my help, you can figure it out yourself, " Ira says before diving into the deep without me.

"Ira, wait."

It's too late, he's gone, and now he's annoyed. Why is Wai so angry with me, I ponder. She's been haunting my dreams for weeks and begging me to hurry. I did my best to find her swiftly. Ira had his mating rituals to fulfil, and perhaps I could have travelled ahead without him. Still, I'm not convinced that would've changed the outcome. If I hadn't gone to Walu, I wouldn't have known where Wai was. I could have sailed the ocean for years while her bones lay behind the rocks. The thought makes me shudder.

Maybe she believes I spent time rescuing Savani and Isa instead of her. But that's not true because they were part of my escape plan. They've also been coaxing Wai back to health, so I'm irritated she's ungrateful. Wai has affected me this way since we were children. Her behaviour is perplexing and erratic.

What would Marama do, I wonder? Korero – my mother, would talk to her patient and attempt to understand the cause of her emotional outburst. So, that's what I must do. I'm petrified. Sailing to Walu was less daunting because I knew what awaited me.

Savani isn't blind. She sees Wai has unsettled me and that the girl is recovering but unhappy.

"Greetings, Wai. My name is Savani, daughter of Vaka-toi and Manui, a descendant of the wind, and I am from the Lagoon of Light. In the name of my ancestors, I offer you my hand in friendship," she states.

The formal introduction is a wise choice by Savani as Wai is well brought up and knows she must respond accordingly. When Wai finishes her introduction, Savani grins, beckons Isa over with food, and introduces her daughter.

Her appetite awakens, and Wai is ravenous. As she consumes her meal, Savani tells their story of how they were taken in a raid and transported to Walu to work and serve Kapanval and his men.

Isa picks up the story of the dancing and when they first met me. Her gratitude and admiration make me sound more heroic than I was.

"If Kai hadn't come, we would have died on Walu. The angry Gods would have destroyed all the women and children. He didn't have to save us from the other men - but he did." She pauses, wipes away a stray tear, and hugs her mother before continuing. "We pretended the three of us were sharing a night of noisy love-making," she giggles with a blush, "but we were pretending and waiting for a chance to escape. The three of us snuck to the beach to launch the waka while an ancestor of Kai hid us from view. It's the most exciting adventure I've ever had in my life," Isa finishes in a rush.

As is the custom of women, the three share food and drinks and discuss their tales and bond. When I return with squid for our next meal, my companions laugh and talk like whanau. Suddenly, I'm awkward and an outsider as I approach them.

I shouldn't have worried. Savani and Isa provided Wai with the explanation she needed for my tardiness.

"Kai! I'm so sorry for my harsh words. Please forgive me?" begs Wai.

She throws her arms around me and hugs me tight against her. I welcome her embrace and stroke her hair like a hurt child. The change in attitude is a relief, but as Wai clings to me, I begin to feel uncomfortable. A discreet cough from Savani saves me from embarrassment, but Isa grins at me and winks.

I hold Wai at arm's length.

"Let me look at you, cousin. You have grown into a lovely young woman. No wonder your parents are desperate for me to return you."

Wai is more beautiful in person than in my dreams. Her eyes are brown, intense, and alive with intelligence. Curly hair cascades in wild waves down her back, streaked to a coppery hue by the sun and sea.

"And you, Kai? Did you also want to find me?"

I know better than to hesitate, but I'm not a good liar, so I answer truthfully.

"You are my cousin, and I was worried about you, so of course. When you visited my dreams, I didn't know who you were, and I was desperate to find you. My only reluctance when I realised the beautiful woman was you is that I would be on the receiving end of your sharp words and pranks." I smile to take the sting out of my honesty.

"Oh, and I proved you right as soon as I could speak."

Wai looks guilty but flashes me a toothy grin of apology. She's stunning, and I grin back like an idiot. No wonder she's left a trail of swooning men behind her. I need to ensure I'm not one of them.

"How do you feel physically? We won't travel until you are ready, even though I know your parents are frantic."

"Kali fortifies me with her strength, so our reconnection will speed my recovery. I'll eat as much as possible, exercise my limbs with Kali and get away from here. I want to go as soon as you're ready to depart."

She takes my hands and searches my face intently. Wai unsettles me and makes me feel uncomfortable in a disturbing way because my body reacts to her proximity. I need korero with Ira, but he's temporarily shut me out.

To my relief, Wai walks to the water, wades into the shallows, and greets Kali in person. They are ecstatic to be together, and restoring their bond is the best healing for Wai.

Savani and Isa are thrilled we'll soon depart and burst into song and dancing while preparing the squid and tidying the camp. It's Nani who comes to my rescue.

"What ails you mokopuna?" she asks.

"I'm confused, Nani. I'm supposed to find a mate, but Wai isn't who I had in mind."

"Hmm, she is pretty, loves the sea, and has been waiting for you. What is it about the girl that doesn't satisfy you?" asks Nani.

"We don't get along well, Nani. Wai has a sharp tongue. I imagine meeting a woman and having the kind of relationship my parents have. Complementary skills, nurturing one another, and our children together as partners. Do you believe I set my standards too high? Ira thinks so."

"Remember, Kai, by the time you were old enough to remember, your parents had spent years together. You can't judge any new relationship based on that. It's like comparing a green piece of wood to a seasoned taiaha."

"I know, but I've also met some of the men she spurned. How do I compare and compete with the best the islands have to offer? Will she be disappointed and lash me with her tongue? Do I want to be rejected too? Stories led me to believe that love makes you feel fantastic, which isn't how I feel."

"And how do you think Starman felt? When he met your mother, she desperately held on to her first love – Tane. He didn't give up. Your father was patient and gently coaxed your mother into sharing a relationship and the child, you, with him. At least you compete with the living, not a spirit and memory."

"But Nani, Starman won Marama. I feel like – prey. Who knows why Wai believes I'm the man she wants? When we were children, she humiliated me at every opportunity. I don't understand her current obsession with me, and I don't trust her. I certainly don't love her. My body has a mind of its own, but I've been by myself a while."

"Give her some time, Kai. Get to know the young woman she has become. Children are cruel and hide their insecurities in all sorts of ways. You are both different people. Take your father's path and get to know Wai before you reject her. That is my counsel."

"I'll try, Nani," I sigh.

Marama has drummed into me that Nani is always right, and Nani's saved me twice. I feel better after airing my troubles and go to work preparing for our voyage. The advice will also make the camp and voyage a pleasant place for us all. As I immerse myself in familiar tasks, my heart lifts, and I sing.

As the sun descends toward the ocean, Wai returns with molluscs and seaweed to accompany the squid, slowly cooking over dying coals. Our meal is merry with laughter and singing. Isa and Wai behave like long-lost sisters, fussing over their hair, and comparing singing techniques and dance moves, so Savani and I clean up.

The stars emerge. I've questioned Savani and Isa about their home island's night sky. While their knowledge is limited, their stories are rich with navigation information, and I settle on a course toward an island group on the way to their home. Other navigators told me to expect a friendly welcome and news of the missing women may have spread. After that, I'll return Wai home swiftly as every day is agony for my relatives.

I lie on my back, enjoying my communion with the heavens, pondering the yearning of Ira and the whales to return to Matariki. The movement of the stars centres me. Starman and I supplement the ancestral knowledge we were gifted. We've travelled further south than most, searching for pounamu and the land of snow and ice. The dancing lights in the sky are a sight I'll never forget. If I close my eyes, I still see them.

"Are you planning our voyage?"

Wai drops to the ground and lies on her back beside me.

"Yes, I am. First, we'll make a detour to islands where I hope to find a way for Savani and Isa to go home. We must hurry because your disappearance is distressing your whanau."

She props herself up on her elbow and smiles at me.

"I'm so glad you came to rescue Kali and me. We don't know how to thank you."

Her breath warms my face, and her lips descend toward mine. Time freezes, and my heart skips in my chest, but she plants a sisterly kiss on my forehead. Part of me is relieved, but I am also disappointed. Wai lies down again, close enough for me to feel the warmth of her skin.

"It was Ira who rescued Kali but don't go lavishing him with your kisses, or I will hear about it forever."

"Where is Ira? Kali said she hasn't seen him today."

"Probably feeding and lurking in the deep. We disagreed, and Ira is making me suffer."

"What do you and a whale disagree about?" she giggles. "Kali and I never argue."

"We don't normally either, but he does tease me mercilessly. I'm definitely little brother."

"Kali and I are the same age, more like twin sisters. It's so good to feel each other again. I was completely lost without her."

"I know how you feel. Ira and I lost contact when a sleep enchantment overcame him. I was frantic. He's such a part of me. Time for me to apologise for being so sensitive to his teasing when he was trying to help."

"That doesn't sound like you, Kai. You've always been good at everything. The golden child of Marama, Starman, and the spirit of Tane the Brave – what could get under your skin?" she laughs.

I'm grateful it's dark, and she can't see the colour of my face.

"Just something stupid. I'm over it now, probably just tired, I suspect."

Chapter 16

Children of Tangaroa

Ira is connected to me but refuses to communicate.

"Ira, I'm sorry."

I throw my thoughts out there, hoping he'll forgive my outburst but he makes me suffer a bit longer. However, I've apologised, and I can feel he misses me.

Wai wants to understand where we're going, so I patiently show her the stars to navigate us to our first destination. She asks many questions, and I'm impressed with her grasp of star maps. There's more to Wai than a pretty face, but I want more from a mate than a tingle of attraction.

We stroll back to camp, discussing the prevailing winds and tides. As we arrive, Isa throws us a smug look and grins at her mother. Aue! That's all I need, a waka full of women determined to make kumara grow on a bare rock.

Bubbles of laughter roll through me like exhaled breath underwater as Ira's amusement with my dilemma escapes him.

"So, you can't live without me because where else can you get entertainment and adventure like this?" I chuckle.

"Your mating dance is more complicated than mine, Kai. If I make a mistake, and I have, I can choose another mate and improve my pursuit next season. Kali told me Wai has impossibly high standards, so not much different to you."

"Then why does Wai believe she had to wait for me?"

"I don't know. But, I tried to help by telling Kali you're a little slow for your age."

"Ira – you're supposed to be on my side."

"Ok, next time we talk, I'll tell her you're stupid and lazy."

"Is this your idea of being helpful?"

"Well, you say you don't want Wai as a mate, so I portray you as unworthy. I'm your brother Kai, and I'm trying to support your decision even when I don't understand it."

"What don't you understand?"

"Why you aren't interested in the mate everyone else is pursuing? There must be something desirable about her."

"She is beautiful, and Wai is the daughter of a chief."

"So she's attractive and has status."

"I suppose so, Ira."

"Wai also has Kali, a sister gifted from Tangaroa, just as you have me. Do you think that makes her valuable as well?"

"Of course. Here, in the islands, they live in the arms and at the mercy of Tangaroa. You're correct as usual."

"And, I'm surprised you rejected her before you met. You both understand the shared bond. Nani gives wise counsel. Get to know Wai, and we'll support your decision if you're sure she isn't a worthy mate."

"Ira, you know she threw a bowl at me when she saw Savani and Isa?"

Ira laughs again and takes me rolling in the deep. "An unfortunate error, and I believe she's apologised."

My parents raised me well, and I know better than to argue with Nani and Ira. The truth is they're usually right. I'm the youngest and have less life experience. Being friendly with Wai, now we're older, shouldn't be difficult, and I must take her home. Her impossibly high standards will most likely ensure she discards me before we arrive. Then I will continue my search for the girl who will hook me, gasping like a prize fish. The thought makes me smile and whistle as I bank the fire.

The placid ocean is glossy with light as we finish stowing our supplies. Ira and Kali languish in warm waters, anxious for us to join them. I dedicate extra attention to the departure karakia, conscious that I carry three women, the life nurturers of Papatūānuku.

Tūatea knifes through the water, eager to run with the tide into our next voyage. Wai sits stiff and proud, looking forward as if to wipe the island prison from her memory. The tantalising promise of returning home excites Savani and Isa. They are full of songs, smiles, and jokes as we sail away, and Kali porpoises around the waka celebrating while Ira shows off flapping his flippers.

I assign each person duties on the voyage. Living in close proximity on a crowded waka requires teamwork and clear lines of communication. Women in the islands grow up with the ocean, and Savani, Isa and Wai are skilled. I teach them what I can about voyaging to pass the time and keep them entertained.

Isa practices new knots with dextrous fingers and splices ropes for me. There's nothing I can teach Wai about fishing, for Kali taught her well, but her love of the stars means she joins me to navigate each night. Our love of kai means Savani, and I exchange recipes and enjoy a friendly competition to create different food with our voyage fare.

We stop to harvest coconuts on atolls and enjoy hot, cooked food. The moon traces an arc through the night sky, casting her silvery net upon the sea. My travel companions never tire of my stories of the heavens, ocean, and wind. Wai takes up my habit of napping during the day so she can navigate with me at night. Her voice is melodious, and she sings many songs of the sea to Kali and Ira as we sail.

Isa is on the lookout and spots islands in the distance.

"Look, look – I can see a big island!"

Ira explored them the night before, but we didn't want to spoil the surprise or excitement for Savani and Isa. Wai grins at me conspiratorially as Kali keeps her well informed, and Savani's smile is accompanied by a tear, for she recognises where we are.

"You're a genius, Kai. I know this island. My Aunty moved here with her man, a navigator, and they'll be able to take us home. Thank you so much."

Mother and daughter sit at the front of Tūātea, straining to catch the first glimpse of the familiar village. Home is no longer somewhere they hope for but a nearby reality. As the palm trees grow in our field of vision, the women sing passionate thanks to their ancestors for guiding them through the darkness.

Isa and Wai fuss over their appearance because they want to make a good impression. Since my lecture from Ira, I attend to my grooming every day, but I rebind my hair and oil my salty limbs.

People fishing are the first to notice us, and a vessel glides ashore to alert the village to expect visitors. When we arrive, curious villagers line up to greet us, so our welcome party swells by the minute. The villagers give us a traditional and respectful welcome. Relatives of Savani and Isa wipe tears from smiling faces, evidence of their relief. Islanders know that when people are taken to Walu, their family never sees them again, so our appearance is a welcome surprise.

Everyone wants to hear our story, but hospitality dictates that we must be fed, housed and allowed to bathe. The Head Man and Woman invite the relatives and us to eat with them in private, giving them a chance to question us and understand the circumstances of our escape and arrival. A sensible leadership decision if Kapanval and his angry raiders are in pursuit of us.

A tower of strength on our voyage, Savani finally gives in to her fraught emotions and is lovingly comforted by her relatives and Isa. My eyes mist because I miss my whanau, especially my mother and Wai quietly takes my hand. She's been without her family for a long time.

The food is a welcome distraction, and our hostess herds us to the eating mat. Dishes prepared on land by someone else are a treat for us, and we eat and drink appreciatively.

A hush descends, and it's time for us to share our tales. Isa and Savani distress the listeners with the sad story of their abduction by the Walu raiders. Although they've had a horrible experience, they are at least alive, and not everyone is as fortunate.

Wai captivates the audience, weaving troughs and crests into the tale of her woes. The heartbreak of believing Kali was dead, elicits a sniff from a sympathetic listener. She's an accomplished storyteller, and everyone leans in as events unfold until Wai passes out from hunger and thirst behind the rock.

I compress my voyage from Aotearoa and concentrate on the fallout from Wai's disappearance. When I describe the worry of my aunt and uncle, Wai looks guilty. She paddled off without telling anyone where she was going. The audience's eyes widen as I recount my arrival on Walu. Still, I save the competition stories for later, speak about meeting Kapanval and the first time I saw Savani and Isa.

The women take up the story of imprisonment on Walu, dancing for their lives and how horrified Savani was when I chose Isa. It's different hearing of that night from another perspective. Isa delights in describing the pretence of our night of passion, and the humour provides welcome relief for our audience before she launches into our harrowing escape.

"Did they chase you?" asks the Head Man.

I must alleviate his concern.

"No, they didn't because offended Gods and angry spirits destroyed them."

Everyone starts asking questions at once until the Head Woman holds up her hand for silence and gestures for me to continue.

And so, I recount an abbreviated version of the clashes between my whanau and Walu. The nods of elders confirm they know some of the stories. It's the same when I tell of rescuing Wai from the blood spirit. I keep Nani and Tane to myself, only alluding to assistance from my ancestors because they, and Ira, are silent allies.

As we finish our shared tale of sighting their island, they dance and drum in appreciation, sending the rest of the village into a frenzy.

We know we'll have to entertain the village tonight by telling our stories again, but that's the role of guests. Everyone is eager for news of other islands, the health and happenings of relatives, and excitement. Savani, Isa, and Wai are shown where they will sleep and the women take them to bathe.

The Head couple retain me a bit longer because they realise I've travelled extensively looking for Wai. They also seek reassurance that vengeful spirits don't pursue us, and I provide them with enough detail to satisfy them.

With food in my puku, my body demands rest, so our hosts find me a quiet place to sleep. Navigators sleep when they can on land because they know the waves won't call them to action. After a quick dip in the lagoon to cleanse my body and mumbled karakia of thanks, my mat awaits.

The evening feast is marvellous. Isa, Wai, and I, cause a stir of excitement among the island's young people, and they compete for our attention. I'm used to giggling girls, and Wai attracted almost every eligible male in the islands, so Isa enjoys it the most. Soon a circle of boys and girls her age cluster around her.

An attractive young woman singles me out during the dancing, reminding me how long I've been at sea. Her teasing smile and the complicated movement of her hips captivate me, so she grabs me to dance at the first opportunity.

"Is she the mate you're seeking, little brother?" Ira asks.

"Not now, Ira; this is a tricky dance," I respond.

"Oh, it will definitely be more complicated now," he laughs.

I wonder what he means and concentrate on what I'm doing. There's no harm in having some fun on land while I'm able. When I return to my place, I find the young men of the village waiting on Wai, who has turned on a charm I didn't know she possessed. She certainly has a gorgeous smile, and to my astonishment, she's polite and attentive.

Will Uncle be impressed if Wai chooses a handsome boy without any wealth, I wonder? Her parents will be happy to see her regardless, but I decide to keep an eye on Wai. She's more flirtatious than I remember. However, it's been years since we saw each other, so I don't know what grown-up Wai is usually like.

We all enjoy the food, drink, dancing, and company. Eventually, people gather around us, anticipating the telling of our story. They've already gleaned from the privileged few who have heard it that our tales are astounding. Artists, drummers, and entertainers are eager to listen and find inspiration for their creations.

Nobody is disappointed. Like all good storytellers, we kept detail in reserve to entertain those who dined with us. The audience is jubilant when they hear of the demise of Kapanval and Walu, and we wait for the dancing to finish before continuing. Drumming and dancing start again after I tell of rescuing Wai. We are all pulled into the celebratory melee of laughing villagers, determined to impress us.

The young dancer who claimed me earlier pulls me out of the firelight and into her arms. With smooth oiled skin, breath sweet and warm, she draws me closer. Every cell in my body wants to be with her, but I can no longer see Wai, and she's my responsibility until I take her home.

I gently prise the girl from me, like separating paua from a rock, and I kiss the top of her head in a brotherly fashion. She pouts at the rejection, announcing her disappointment without speaking, but I place my arm around her shoulder, and we rejoin the dancing mass.

Isa makes a surprised face and waggles her finger at me, laughing. She would be firm friends with my sister Aroha in a heartbeat, and I make a face at her as I dance by, joining the safety of the men drumming.

My father taught me to drum on our first trip to the islands, and I practiced with the other boys my age whenever I could. Starman was probably relieved to find an outlet on land for my boundless energy because, at home, my mother always kept me busy. When the drumming ends with a triumphant shout, everyone slumps to the ground, laughing, breathless from the exertion.

Only Wai wears a frown, her admirers forgotten. She stares off into the dark as if straining to hear a faint voice.

"You look worried."

"It's Kali; she has a feeling. A misgiving that all isn't as it should be with her pod. I don't know how else to explain it, but she's reaching. I must go to her."

"Wait, I don't want to be rude, so I'll tell our hosts and come with you."

"What? Afraid some good-looking man will accompany me into the shadows?" she asks.

I feel Ira smirking, smug in the background, so I shut him out.

"No, of course not. Why do you always think the worst of me?"

Making straight for our hosts, I let them know Wai is worried and we're going to the beach. They burst into laughter and wave me on my way, holding their bellies, for tonight, I'm the source of amusement for everybody.

Wai has already left, and I jog to catch up with her as her entourage of admirers strain to see where she's gone. She wades into the water, chittering for Kali. The dolphin darts into view and rolls onto her back, waving her flippers at Wai.

"Ira, do you know what's bothering Kali?"

"So now you're talking to me?"

"Please, Ira, enough of the teasing torture. Can you shed any light on why Kali is upset?"

"Her pod isn't where she expected them to be, and they're out of her communication range. I'm trying to help, but I don't know which pod is hers. We should help her."

"I was planning on leaving tomorrow anyway because Wai needs to go home. Maybe we can find the pod on our way?"

"Let the girl know. She knows how anxious Kali is."

Wai spends a long time in the water with Kali, so patiently, I wait for her to come ashore. She's surprised to find me sitting on the sand, contemplating the stars and singing softly.

"Still guarding me like a prize fish, Kai?"

"Actually, Ira and I decided to leave early tomorrow, to try and help Kali find her pod. Can you be ready to leave just after the sun rises so we can catch the morning tide?"

"Oh, yes, that would be great. Thanks to you and Ira. Kali means the world to me. I know you and Ira understand us and the bond we share."

Wrapping her arms around me, Wai rests her head on my shoulder and sighs. Tonight two beautiful young women embrace me, and regrettably, I go to my mat alone. Positively, I will sleep well, so I kiss the top of my cousin's curly head and lament lost opportunities.

Our hosts are disappointed our stay is short but understand the urgency to relieve my relatives' worries. I arise in the dark hours of the morning to complete spiritual preparations for our journey.

The young men smitten with Wai arrive at sunrise to help, along with Savani, Isa and a giggling group of unattached women. Isa extolled my virtues to entertain her new friends, inflaming my admirers' desire for my company. The preparations keep me busy, but the more I ignore them, the more they try to help and get in the way.

One of the village aunties arrives to save me. She swiftly assigns the girls chores elsewhere and shoos them off with a flick of her hand. I smile my thanks at her, and she inclines her head graciously. In my village, our elders also monitor behaviour and exercise authority when appropriate, and the youngsters obey.

With Tūātea loaded, and the tide turning, it's time to say our goodbyes. Savani and Isa cry. Their tears flow with gratitude, the bitterness of losing friends, empathy for our relatives, and an acknowledgement of the difficult path we travelled together. For Isa, there's also a tinge of regret that her adventure is over.

"I'm sure Isa is destined for more adventures," chuckles Nani.

"I agree – there are some creatures born with a destiny," agrees Ira.

As if Isa heard my companion's comments, she takes me aside and whispers. "If things don't work out with Wai, or you need someone to voyage with, I'm almost grown. You know where to find me don't you?"

I nod, laugh, and rumple her hair. Savani and Isa help us launch Tūātea, and they wade into the lagoon, determined to keep us in view as long as possible.

Chapter 17

Harbingers of Change

When we hit the deep, Ira surfaces nearby and flaps his tail while Kali darts around the waka. I wear my love for the sea on my face, there's a joy that consumes me whenever I return to the ocean, and I belt out sailing songs. Wai laughs as Kali splashes her, as happy as I to be upon the waves and close to her kaitiaki. She joins in the singing when she knows the song, and when Ira adds his melancholic whalesong to our voices, we close our eyes to savour the magic.

Ira located the two pods of dolphins closest to where Kali was expecting to find her pod. The first course I set will place us between them, and we hope Kali can identify her kin. Kali has been missing for a while, and they may have assumed the worst. As I work the paddle, Wai sits quietly, enjoying the peace and freedom.

"You look happy, Wai. Are you excited to be going home?"

"I'm happy, Kai, for now. I am free. You don't understand what it's like being a woman; born to be traded like a pearl or a fine waka."

"No, I don't. I know my mother felt the same as you when she was young. Marama is highly respected in Aotearoa for her healing abilities and connection to the spirits."

"Your mother sounds like a talented woman. Unfortunately, I don't have those kinds of skills. My assets are my father's status, a pretty face, and friendship with the most beautiful creature in the whole world."

"A connection to Tangaroa through his children is a unique asset. You're the only person I know, who isn't a son of the sea, that has been gifted a bond. That's a special gift."

"I suppose so. I never thought of it like that. People look at us and discuss me as if I'm a possession. Yes, I ran away to find Kali, but I also tried to escape my fate, which didn't work out so well."

"Is that why you were desperate for me to come - to rescue you from your fate?"

"I guess so. You were voyaging when still a boy and have had a life of adventure while I stayed at home fishing in the lagoon, growing taro, and making baskets. I don't expect you to understand, Kai, but I want more – I want a future."

Wai frowns as she turns away, deep in thought, watching clouds scud lazily across the sky. Marama, Isa, and Wai have expressed similar feelings as girls and young women. I wonder what my life would have looked like if I was a girl. There's no way I would sail around the islands in my waka, so I'm pleased to be a man and a son of the sea. I respect women. They are the keepers of life, builders of whakapapa, and beloved of Papatūānuku, the mother of us all. But, the nature of their role as nurturers does constrain their lives. I haven't thought about it much because Marama and Aroha are leaders in our village. Our spirit guides and healers traditionally choose a partner themself.

Suddenly, I feel sorry for Wai because her fate isn't hers to determine. Most matches for people of status are made by parents and elders for alliance and trade. Like my mother, Wai is curious, but her beauty promises attractive children who may also be blessed by Tangaroa. When Aroha is your sister, you know better than to offer a feisty female a bowl of pity.

"You are thoughtful, little brother."

"I thought Wai harboured a girlish dream of us, being together. Now, I understand that she wants to escape. The future planned for her isn't to her liking."

"Ah, so she has much in common with your mother."

"Yes, she does."

"So, perhaps she is more suitable as a mate?"

"I didn't say that, Ira. Wai's desire for me is fuelled by her lust for adventure and freedom – not love."

"Did she say that?"

"No, she didn't, but apart from attaching herself like a paua a couple of times, Wai hasn't shown any signs of love."

"Aue! Kai. How many times have you been in love?"

"Well, never, but-"

"Ah! Just as I thought. You're searching for something when you don't know what it is."

"That's not fair, Ira. I'm seeking what my parents have because I grew up surrounded by their love for each other."

"That's akin to wanting someone else's unique eyes, Kai, or growing a tree that looks exactly the same as another. Nature doesn't work that way."

"Now, now, are you two squabbling again?" sighs Nani.

"No, Nan. I know better than to argue with either of you. I'm keeping an open mind about Wai – I promise."

"Hmph, that's not how it sounds to me," Ira grumbles.

"I'm sorry, Ira, but sometimes I feel you exaggerate her attributes because you want me to choose a mate. We're getting along much better – as cousins."

"That may be true, Kai. I've become fond of Kali and Wai but promised not to interfere, so I'll keep my thoughts to myself."

"Don't shut me out, though," I plead.

"That's as horrible for me as it is for you, so I won't."

"Nani, do you know which pod Kali is looking for?" I ask to change the subject.

"No, I don't mokopuna. Keep to your course and plan because I cannot think of anything better."

Wai has given me a lot to ponder, but nothing diminishes my good mood on a fine day at sea. She's learned to manage the paddle well, so we take turns while the weather is good, and I nap. My ability to fall asleep at will surprises Wai, but new parents develop the same skill for the same reason I tell her, – necessity. If the weather turns stormy, I can't rest. She nods sagely, concentrates on maintaining the course with help from Kali and the day slides by.

"Kai, wake up! I need to show you something."

The shaking I get from Wai snaps me to alert. She drags me to the side of the waka, hands shading her eyes, and points to the horizon. My eyes are accustomed to scanning the ocean and I immediately spot a dot in the distance. Some kind of waka, and it's large, so I scramble to pull the sail down because I don't want them to see us. There is a rolling swell that is perfect for hiding us from view.

"Who do you think it is, Kai? Surely, not more raiders."

"I don't know Wai, so I prefer they don't see us. That waka is enormous. I'm going to take a look with Ira. Keep us on this course if you can, but if we drift, don't worry; I'll be back soon.

My brother is feeding in the other direction, but he answers my call, and we merge.

"Nani, can you see the waka on the horizon? Do you know if they are friendly or not?" I ask.

"Aue! Mokopuna, they are the harbingers of change to our world. I cannot see their spirits, but they are raiders, unlike any we have known. Take a look at the enemy that will come, but stay out of sight," she whispers.

When the whales meet in Rangitāhua, they discuss everything happening in the sea. Ira knows of the many people who voyage, searching for riches and adventure. The vessel Wai spotted isn't alone, and Ira tells me they traverse the ocean regularly to trade.

We speed through the water, and Ira takes a big breath before diving deep. The waka are impressive, as long as the kauri trees in the north, and they are nearly as high. There are three waka in the fleet, and I'm curious to know what they are trading.

"Nani, can you see anything on the waka?"

"Many people with hairy faces and strange garments, climbing and pulling ropes to work the sails. I've never seen such a big waka. They are greedy, violent people without proper Gods," she grumbles.

"Scars will be inflicted on Papatūānuku, the domain of Tangaroa polluted, and the children of Tane crash and burn – Aue!" Nani laments.

Nani delivers a prophecy I don't want to hear, and I shudder involuntarily in response. Ira has alluded to the challenges our descendants will face in the future when the tribes of the north invade the south. I comprehend the urgency of his matchmaking, for he and Nani see the storm approaching.

"Ira, can we go closer? I want to look at their paddle and the design of the waka."

Curiosity overrides my misgivings, and we have a good look. The wood is different but beautifully crafted and fitted together with a waterproof substance. While I can't see the navigator, the paddle functions like mine, and I can see an anchor. We move away so Ira can breathe but make several forays to examine the vessels, which are all of a similar design.

"Nani, can I travel with you for a look as you once travelled with your guide scouting Kāingatipu?"

"Yes, but you must prepare yourself, and I will take you from dreaming."

I return to my body, and when I open my eyes, Wai is staring at me.

"What did you see?"

"An evil omen and the winds of change," I sigh.

She looks so worried, I recount what Ira and I observed, but there's no way to soften the prophecy. When I tell her I want a closer look, Wai throws her arms around me with eyes squeezed shut.

"Wai, don't fret; Nani will take me in a dream. I must prepare myself with karakia, but can you paddle and take care of my body?"

A twinkle of mischief flits across her face, and I immediately regret assigning my care to her. Who knows what Wai plans but with tasks to do, I don't torture myself wondering.

The role of a spirit guide is new to me, and I'm excited to travel with Nani. I follow her instructions meticulously and supplement her tasks with my rituals. Wai prepares a hearty meal to provide the energy the spirit world burns and makes enough so I can eat when I return. She naps while I take the paddle and readjust our course when the moon and first stars emerge.

Laying on my mat, I slide into dream where Nani greets me. She has transformed into a spirit bird, and with a blink, I see through her eyes. Soaring through the heavens, we descend to hover above the boats. The detail is sharp and clear. I observe the many sails, the pattern of their placement, and the rigging, and I watch the men on the deck. While I can't understand what they are saying, I note their actions in response.

The smaller waka are pursuing the larger one but cannot catch it. The large waka isn't able to outrun the smaller ones. The vessels are engaged in a battle.

What terror is this, I wonder? Clouds of smoke and fire spew from cylindrical beasts that fling projectiles at the other waka. I've never seen such weapons. Men scramble in teams around the cylinders, preparing them in a highly coordinated effort that I find riveting. Their actions speak of many hours of training, so I assume what they're doing are critical tasks of war.

The distance between them narrows suddenly before the large waka swings around, changing course, and unleashes a barrage of missiles at the closing craft. A pursuing waka loses a mast. Then the other tilts to one side after a projectile punctures its side. My assumption is confirmed; the cylinders are their weapons.

I'm eager to move closer to see how they work and the role each man plays. They fill them with black powder, which I'm certain makes the smoke and fire because I see them light it. The battle is gruesome. Men lie broken and injured while blood and guts slick the wood. The pursuing waka are crippled, one is sinking, and it appears the large vessel has won the battle.

The men have brown skin like us but are hairy, and most wear similar garments. Some have things on their heads and what I assume are weapons hanging from their belts. They don't use them. I suppose because the waka are far apart.

One man has a shining ring dangling from his ear, and he looks straight up into the night sky, perceives us in the spirit world, and hastily pulls an object from his shirt - tohunga. Nani and I are gone before his hand moved.

I awake on my mat, starving. Wai cuddles against me, and my anatomy is excited by the sensation.

"What are you doing? You're supposed to be paddling," I splutter.

"In one of your stories, you spoke of having an anchor in the physical world – so that's what I am for you. Are you hungry?"

I'm grateful it's dark, and she can't see I'm hungry for more than food.

"Never been so ravenous in my life," I reply.

Wai scurries to the leftovers and brings me a smoked fish, prawns, a roasted bird, coconut, taro, kumara, seaweed, and nectar cakes from the island. I eat greedily, wash it all down with coconut water and lick my fingers. Her eyes grow large as I consume more and more food. When I belch, she giggles.

"That was ridiculous, Kai. I've never seen anyone eat that much before." She puts her hand over her mouth to stop laughing, but it doesn't work. The terrible thing is - I'm still hungry. "So, how was it? What did you see? What kind of people are they?"

"If you get me some more food – I'll tell you."

"No! Are you serious?"

I nod at her and rub my belly. With a disbelieving shake of her head, she gets me another smoked fish. Between mouthfuls, I tell Wai what I saw and when I get to the part where the tohunga sees us – she covers her face with her hands. Recounting the information is good for me to retain the detail. I don't know why, but I feel it's significant.

"The noise and battle disturb everything in the sea."

"Do you think Kali's pod may have been scared by them?"

"There's no way to be sure, but it's possible. Two waka were chasing another, but the pursued vessel changed course and attacked not long after we arrived. Who knows how long they were fighting."

While I thought I was gone for a few minutes, the stars tell a different story, and it's early morning. Although Wai lay on the mat with me, we remained almost on course, so I make few adjustments. Weary limbs are heavy, but the full puku makes me content. Wai snatched a bit of sleep, so she offers to take the first shift. I fall asleep upright where I'm sitting.

I'm on a rock, painted with rainbow colours but surrounded by the sea. An elderly woman sits cross-legged, weaving flax, opposite me.

"The people of the north move closer Kai. You and Ira must help turn the first wave from Aotearoa, or our people will perish."

"Is this a dream? Where did you come from?"

"We have met before. Manaia is my name – grandmother of Nani and your sister's guide. Hold fast to your knowledge of their waka."

The sensation of falling jerks my head up, and I wake. It's dark, and Wai is next to me, working the paddle. I repeat the dream conversation to myself several times and signal Wai to get some rest. The comforting presence of the paddle in my hands soothes me, and the movement of Tūātea centres my world. Marama and Nani, when she lived, both experienced dream messages, but I'm green wood – barely harvested and not yet seasoned.

"Kai, are you troubled?" Nani asks.

"The spirit world is new to me, Nan, and I'm worried I'll do something wrong. When you speak to me as Ira does, it's familiar. I just had my first dream experience. Your grandmother, Manaia, sat weaving flax on a rock under a rainbow and spoke to me. Not what I expected when I fell asleep."

"If Manaia visited your dream, there's important information our ancestors want you to know. What did she say?"

"The people of the north move closer. Ira and I must help turn the first wave from Aotearoa, or our people will perish. Hold fast to my knowledge of their waka."

"Make sure you commit the words to memory, Kai. You'll understand the significance of the prophecy when the time comes."

"How long does it take? Do I need to stay awake tonight, or will this happen in a turn of seasons or three?"

"The strands of the future are always weaving, but because the ancestors mentioned you and Ira, it will happen in your lifetime."

"That's not very helpful, Nan. Can you be more specific?"

"No, I can't, Kai. Time flows to different tides across the realms. But, you must recall every detail of the waka you observed with Ira and me. Now, we must begin your training – you are late to the hangi," she chuckles.

Chapter 18

Acceptance

Nani is intent on making up for lost years of training. I believe I'm a fast learner with a good memory, but she challenges me to be better. Many karakia are familiar because I've listened to my mother from the womb, but I realise my whakapapa must extend through many lines back to creation.

I'm training muscles that I've barely exercised before, so they're weak. I dream travel every day with Nani, so we strengthen our bond separate from Ira and venture into the spiritual realm together. Perhaps my genes are comfortable in unfamiliar territory because I thrive under her tutelage.

The training and navigation consume hours of my time, so I'm grateful Wai has Kali for company. Ira confesses he misses me, which makes me happy. Wai proves a useful travel companion by taking a shift at the paddle, fishing, making kai and repairing ropes. We slip into a comfortable companionship because the freedom of voyaging exhilarates her. Wai is a different person because she's cheerful and smiles, so I barely recognise her.

We are low on coconuts and crave hot food, so we beach Tūātea on an atoll. Wai splashes me in the shallows, so I throw her over my shoulder and dump her in the water. She surfaces, spluttering and laughing while Kali chitters her amusement nearby. On the beach, Wai trips me and covers me with sand, so I pull her to the ground and repay the favour.

It's good to laugh together and behave like children. I'm pleased we're getting along well. We plunge into the small lagoon to remove the sand before lighting a fire. I want to make my mother's fish stew, and Wai wants the kina and soft seaweed Kali found for her.

"Can we sleep here tonight, Kai? I know you're in a hurry to take me home, but I love voyaging, and so does Kali. She and Ira will power ahead on the search while we sleep because the pods are near. Please, can we sleep on the ground?" she begs.

The prospect attracts me as my lessons are sometimes exhausting, and Nani agrees we need rest. Wai is ecstatic, hugs me, and immediately runs to haul gear ashore to make camp, so I shake my head laughing and help her. Maybe we can just be cousins from now on.

As Wai brings her comb and treasures from the beach, the sun fires her curly hair, a smile beams from inside her and – she is the girl of my dreams.

I swallow uncomfortably at the admission as the advice from Ira replays.

"You look thoughtful. Dreaming of our feast stretchy puku?" Wai asks.

"Ah, yes, I am. And looking forward to your kina – one of my favourite kaimoana."

"Kali is waiting for me. See you soon. I can almost taste them," she giggles.

Watching her lithe form plunge into the sea, I realise Wai has ceased pursuing me. I wonder if her desperation for me to arrive was interwoven with her escape plan. Maybe Wai is a woman who doesn't need a man, prefers women or is content with Kali as a companion, the same way I enjoy being with Ira.

My feelings for Wai have grown. I like her and need to be cautious I don't become another rejected admirer, because I'm conscious I must find a mate. Sailing the ocean in my waka isn't conducive to meeting attractive women, but once Wai is home, I can be more sociable.

Maybe I can try the whale strategy and breed as many young as possible – now that makes me laugh. Our old Chief at home swears a man with many women has many problems; by all accounts, he had both so he knows. I must apply myself to finding a mate as I've done to learn new skills. Only one face swims in my mind and haunts my dreams - Wai.

We work well together, and our make-shift camp wafts delicious cooking aromas. It's like we're the only people in the world. There's a contentment in Wai I never noticed before. She breaks open her haul of sea urchins, slurping the rich tongues of roe with relish.

"I thought we were eating those later, Wai."

"Esteemed navigator, I need to sample your food before I serve it," she giggles. "Without your service, I may drift on the ocean lost forever. Now there's a thought — can I offer you a rotten kina?"

Her teasing doesn't put me off. I 'help' her with the shelling by sampling each one until Wai shoos me away. I'm not offended because my mother and Aroha also find my propensity to eat more kina than I shell annoying. Chastised, I return to my chores and sample my fish stew which isn't as good as Marama's, so I keep adding ingredients.

When we can wait no longer, we enjoy a long leisurely meal, starting with the kina and savouring the salty warm food Wai has missed. There is tender young coconut to eat afterwards, and I make tea with one of Marama's unique blends. Wai laughs at my stories and tells me hilarious tales. She's relaxed, and our evening is fun.

"If only we could stay here forever," she sighs.

"Won't you be happy to see your whanau?"

"Yes, I will. I've missed them. But what will come after our reunion makes me want to stay here, where I'm free. I don't suppose you'd leave me here with Kali?"

"You know I can't. I promised your parents I would bring you home. What are you afraid of? Maybe you'll find happiness."

"Do you really want to know?"

"Yes, or I wouldn't have asked, silly."

"It's difficult to explain. My whole life, I've felt that Kali and I are waiting for our – our purpose. We both know we have a destiny, but what exactly that is, we don't understand yet. Do you think I'm delusional?"

"No, I don't. But how can you be sure that your destiny isn't awaiting you with one of your admirers? Perhaps your purpose is linked to someone else."

Wai darts a sharp look at me.

"Very perceptive of you, Kai. Kali and I dream together sometimes and – never mind."

"And, what? What do you dream of?"

"Promise not to laugh at me." Wai looks like a naughty child for a moment.

"I promise."

She still hesitates, and her skin colours, blushing.

"We dream of you, Kai. Always of you. A relentless succession of scenes from the past and, I think, the future. That's how I came to you and asked you to hurry. I needed you to save me, then Kali disappeared, and I was desperate for help. And you came." A frown creases Wai's brow, and she looks thoughtful. "Somehow, our lives are inextricably linked."

"So, you believe I'm part of your destiny?"

"Kali, Ira and I know you are. Kai, you've already shaped the path of my life by rescuing me, but what comes next? Nobody knows. Thanks for not laughing at me. Apparently, my imagination has always been wild."

"Dreams can be gifts, warnings or prophetic burdens, so they are never a laughing matter. You've given me much to think about, Wai."

I haven't considered that Wai and I may have a destiny together that doesn't have anything to do with mating. Foolishness on my part to be fixated on one outcome. Perhaps Wai has a calling as a spirit guide and needs to return with me so Marama can teach her. Or there could be a task not yet revealed. Aue! The possibilities are endless, and Nani won't return until tomorrow. Ira is busy hunting for Kali's pod with the dolphin, so I default to contemplating the heavens.

"Come, Wai," I hold out my hand, "let's see if the stars have any answers for us."

When her hand grasps mine, a tingling sensation invades my fingers, hand, arm and then the rest of my body. She glances up at me, and I know Wai feels it too. I don't have to look at the heavens to know my destiny and Wai's are linked. I suddenly feel vulnerable. Whether I take her home or not is irrelevant. Wai is in my life.

As we lie on the ground, still holding hands, I point out constellations that are difficult to find. Have our heartbeats synchronised? My body has a rhythmic pulse, and it feels like our blood is flowing through our bodies as if we are one being.

The heavens erupt in a spectacular display of light bursts. I've seen these phenomena before, with Starman on our voyage to his first home. Wai beams at me, eyes wide in wonder, and her pleasure illuminates her face.

She's so beautiful I forget the heavens for a moment but force my gaze skyward.

I'm in so much trouble, I admit. Despite all my denials, I'm as captivated by Wai as any of her tribe of admirers. But now, it's worse because I like her, and she isn't pursuing me out of lust. There's nothing I can do to influence the weaving strands of fate, so I surrender myself to the magic of the moment, letting my foolish heart skip with joy.

Chapter 19

Confusion

I awake and remember a dream of Wai. She's infected me with her affliction and I slap my thighs to stop my pathetic mooching.

"Did you sleep well, little brother?" Ira inquires.

The silkiness of his question makes me wonder if he shared my dream.

"Yes," I respond brusquely, "I did. How was your night? Did you find Kali's pod?"

"No, we didn't. Neither of the close pods is her kin. Something is amiss, Kai. It's not unusual for Kali's pod to forage where the fishing is good, but they frequent the same spots seasonally. Perhaps they're searching for Kali, in which case they could be anywhere."

"We have a difficult decision to make. Take Wai home, so everyone knows she's safe, or continue to pursue the dolphins and let our whanau fret. Time for a serious korero with Wai and Kali. Any advice or thoughts, Ira?"

"I think you choose the right course, little brother. Wai or Kali's relatives suffer either way, so they must decide."

Wai prepares hot food and has water boiling on the fire. She's making the most of our stay on land, but Wai has packed and stowed her sleeping mat. Her smile and greeting make my puku lurch in a weird but pleasant way, but I focus on our critical conversation. I return Wai's smile and take the food she offers me. It smells good, and my puku rumbles, which makes Wai laugh, so we start eating.

"Kali told you she and Ira didn't find her kin?"

"Yes, and she's worried. Do you and Ira have any idea where we should look next? The other fishing grounds they visit, or should we try another direction away from the noisy waka? We aren't sure what else to do."

"The two of you have a difficult decision to make together. You've been missing as long as Kali and your parents sent everyone to search for you before the pod's separation became a concern. Ira and I don't know where Kali's kin are, so we can't tell how long the search will last. Every day we search for Kali's kin is torture for your whanau because they don't know you live. In hindsight, we should have sent a paddler with a message. Each day we delay the search for Kali's pod means anxiety for the dolphins. We can return to the nearest island and ask someone to take a message to our whanau, but we'll lose time from the search and your return. There's also a possibility the pod returned to your home Wai because

Kali spends most of her time with you. I'm sorry, Wai, there's no right or wrong decision here, just choices. I'll stow the rest of the gear and break camp to give you and Kali some time."

I squeeze Wai's shoulder to convey my support, and she raises troubled eyes to mine. With a stoic nod, she walks to the water to be closer to her sister. No matter what they choose, one of them will feel selfish, and I'm grateful the decision isn't mine.

The waka is ready, and so is the tide. Finally, Wai emerges from the water, a vision that steals my breath. Is she a gift from my father, or is that wishful thinking? Wai isn't smiling and looks pale.

"Are you ok, cousin?" I ask.

"If being argued into submission by my best friend is ok, I guess I'm fine," she frowns.

"Kali wants to take you home first?"

"Yes, she does. Kali doesn't want my whanau to suffer, believing I'm dead. Like you, she considers the possibility her pod is waiting for her to return to our home."

"Ka pai (well done), we know how tough this choice is."

"But you don't understand, Kai. Once I'm home, I won't be allowed to search with Kali. My whanau won't let me out of their sight, ever again, until they pair me off with some fat old chief," she sobs.

"Don't fret, Wai. Besides, I've met some of your 'fat old chiefs', and they looked more like the pearls of Tangaroa to me. I met Viti."

My sarcastic description of her admirers releases a fresh deluge of tears – aue! We should leave, and I want to comfort Wai.

"Look, when we get home, I'll ask your parents if you can search with me."

"Oh, thank you, thank you, how-"

"I can't promise you they'll agree, but I'll do my best to persuade them, ok?"

"You're clever, Kai, and you have your ancestors and Ira to help us. I have complete faith in you. Thank you so much."

Wai throws her arms around me and crushes me with her hug. If I fail to convince her parents that she should search with me, Wai will be devastated, and I'll have to escape at speed. The prospect of leaving her causes a pang of sadness.

"I felt that," says Ira cheerfully.

We launch Tūātea, and I'm grateful to return to the water where many tasks occupy me. Wai is more cheerful and glances at me with grateful adoration. I'll ask Nani to help me win over my relatives because I can't face letting Wai down.

The wind is brisk and fills the sail with our urgency. We have a destination, and it's good to know where we are going, as the fruitless pursuit of dolphins left us frustrated. After days of voyaging together, Wai and I are a slick team, rejoicing in our vessel's speed.

Kali plays in the wake and bow waves alternately, determined to show Wai her decision is the right one. In the distance, we see Ira breach in a magnificent display, slapping his tail on the surface. Crystal droplets reflect rainbows in the air, leaving us breathless and laughing like children.

Like me, I've noticed Wai is happiest at sea and with Kali. Focusing on our differences blinded me to our undeniable similarities and compatibility, or perhaps my growing attraction to Wai is bending my perceptions. I've never been so confused about my motives and wonder what's happening to me.

The bubbling laughter inside me announces Ira's amusement.

"What, Ira, is so funny?"

"You are, little brother."

"I believe you're experiencing the bite of first love, Kai. Confusion, self-doubt, unusual feelings, unfamiliar emotions, and vulnerability – sound familiar?" Nani asks gently.

I'm eternally grateful Wai isn't privy to our conversation because it's embarrassing, and I'm emotionally naked.

"No need to worry, boy, she can't hear us," says Nani.

"What am I supposed to do, Nan?"

"Carry on. There's no hurry, and taking time to know each other benefits you both. You have learned to respect each other, work together and love one another as cousins. Let your relationship run its natural course. You'll know if she's meant for you, and so will Tangaroa."

"Ira believes he knows already," I respond.

"I didn't say that, Kai. I merely expressed my growing friendship with Kali and Wai, and I promised not to interfere."

"I know, Ira. Sorry, I'm just so touchy at the moment," I shrug.

Wai glances at me, wondering why I'm shrugging my shoulders probably. So, I turn my attention to what I know and where I'm comfortable and urge Tūātea to racing speed. We grin like idiots as we skim across the water, and Wai is content, knowing I will plead for her to accompany me.

The weather is kind to us, with glorious sunny days one after another. At night the heavens are a blaze of stars, and I wonder if Wai enjoys her lessons as much as I do. We huddle together, or I sit behind her, arms encircling her to point out stars of interest. The paddle is shared to steer our course, and our mats move closer together. I watch Wai as she sleeps, and I know she watches me because she tells me when I twitch or snore.

Kali chitters and porpoises beside the waka, and Wai dives in to join her. They keep up because Kali powers herself and Wai through the water. I enjoy excursions with Ira too. He waits until the waka is distant before he surfaces to take me on his back. When we finish our play, Ira drops me ahead so his bulk doesn't disturb Tūātea, and I clamber onto the net at the back as the waka passes.

It's an idyllic life for us all, and nobody wants it to end. But, a speck on the horizon announces our arrival soon enough. Wai becomes tense and snappy but apologises with a sigh.

"I've been dreading this day, Kai, even though I'm dying to see my parents."

Ira and Kali are subdued as the island looms in the distance. Long before we get there, waka sail out to greet us, and when they see Wai, they wave and race home to share the news and we slow to give the islanders time. Drums pound as the village swings into action and prepares to receive their chief's lost daughter. Tears of relief are shed in streams before we land.

"Wai, Wai!" shouts her mother as she wades into the water.

We are still distant from the beach, so Wai dives in, and Kali tows her home. The two women, mother, and daughter embrace. The emotional toll on my aunt is evident in her gaunt face, and I feel guilty. It's not that we took our time, but the past few days lacked urgency and speed. They wade ashore together, arms around one another as if nothing will ever separate them again. Somehow, I'll have to persuade my distraught aunt to let Wai roam again.

I try not to think too far ahead and manoeuvre the waka to where many hands wait to assist me. The familiar mechanical tasks calm me, but Wai has left a void. Ira comforts me, sharing the ocean, which doesn't fill the space, but his reassuring presence soothes me.

The festivities have begun. Girls and women dance on the beach in a hip-shaking celebration while men leap and whoop, slapping their limbs. Many hugs, kisses, and flowers rain down on me as I walk to the communal whare, where I see Aunty, Uncle, and Wai.

Uncle squeezes me like a giant squid before thumping my back so hard I want to cough. Tears roll down his face, and he can't speak. I hug his portly figure which has found Aunty's lost weight. The relief is palpable because he acknowledged they may have lost Wai for good. The thought of never seeing Wai again brings a lump to my throat, so I empathise with his pain.

Eventually, Uncle holds me at arm's length and bellows for food, drink, and cheering. I'm a hero to my relatives. Aunty launches herself at me with weepy thanks flowing from her lips. Wai shrugs and rolls her eyes at me, laughing. She's delighted to see her parents so beholding to me because I'll have a better chance of taking her dolphin hunting.

My Aunt covers her mouth in horror when my puku rumbles like thunder. I am hungry. She places platter after platter of food in front of me, and I consume it with enthusiasm. By now, Wai is used to my hearty appetite, but some girls can't stop giggling. Aunty gives them a friendly whack with her fan, to no avail. Wai glares at them until they stop and apologise for their bad manners. However, my burp of appreciation sets everyone off again.

The afternoon and evening roll into a blur of eating, drinking, hugging, and dancing until a yawn escapes me.

"We're so sorry, Kai, for our lack of manners this visit. The excitement of Wai coming home is overwhelming. Come, someone will show you to the guest whare."

"It's ok, Mama. I'll take Kai to his sleeping mat. After all, it was my rescue that depleted his energy and puku." The wry smile on Wai's face belies her words.

"Well, haven't you grown some manners, Wai," laughs her Mama. "Don't take too long because I can't see enough of you."

An amused smirk flirts with Aunty's mouth. She's wondering if a romance has blossomed between us. Trust her to be so observant.

"Come." Wai takes my hand and leads me from the crowded, noisy whare.

"You're not planning on having your wicked way with me, are you?" I ask in a timid voice.

She throws back her head and laughs.

"Now that you mention it, I have a cunning plan. If my parents believe we might make a match voluntarily, they'll probably throw me on your waka to look for the dolphins."

Wai takes my hands and steers me to the beach, illuminated by an almost full moon, and she pulls me to the sand laying her head on my shoulder. People will see our silhouettes from outside the communal whare. I admit her plan is solid.

"Now, show me the stars you will use to guide you home to Aotearoa. After that, I promise to let you sleep."

As tired as I am, the stars exert their allure, and I can't help but launch into an explanation. At last, I turn to kiss Wai's head and say goodnight.

Wai turns and raises herself off the sand before pulling my head down to kiss my lips. It's like fire searing my mouth. Passion surges in me, I don't want it to end, and Wai has plastered her body against mine.

I push her away. We are in plain view, and I don't want to make a spectacle of ourselves.

"It's not wise to overplay our hand, cousin," I pant. "If we go too far, we'll be matched by the morning."

"You're right as usual," Wai replies, wiping swollen lips. "Come with me. You must sleep alone on your mat where everyone can see you."

My hand is clammy in hers as we walk to the guest whare. People smile at us as we pass by.

"Goodnight, Kai."

Wai squeezes my hand before heading back to her parents. I know sleep will elude me because our kiss is replaying over and over in my mind like a lesson I'm trying to learn. I'm in deep, stormy, and unfamiliar water – aue!

Chapter 20

The Decision

Aunty and Uncle are more attentive in the morning, so the reports of Wai and me on the beach have reached their eager ears. Even I cannot eat the quantity of food offered to me, but I try.

I must ask them to allow Wai to accompany me. Timing is everything. So, after my huge meal, I offer to tell them the tale of Wai's rescue. Their emphatic nods encourage me to speak, but I ask them to take food and drink because the story is long.

While they issue instructions and make themselves comfortable, I consider what to tell of Tane, Nani and Ira. Marama taught me to maintain my mystery and guard our ancestors against scrutiny at a young age. Protecting the identity of our loved ones in the next realm and ensuring Ira isn't hunted to use against me are at the forefront of my mind. They'll collectively become 'the

Ancestors', and I'll be more heroic than I am, but any admiration is advantageous.

It's an emotional experience for my relatives, shared by the three of us. They are the village leaders and need time to compose themselves before a more general telling. While they're entertained by the competition trials Kapanval's men put me through, Aunty sobs when Wai disappears, then howls when I discover a blood spirit possesses her. I throw herbs on the fire and offer karakia to their ancestors in thanks and to fortify them. I comfort them as much as possible, but it's a harrowing tale.

To set the bait, I let my admiration for Wai seep into the story. It isn't difficult because it's true. They exchange glances while I praise her sailing, cooking, cheerful disposition, and ability to set up a camp. I wax lyrical about her affinity to my sea father, Tangaroa, and the blessing of Atua (Gods) is a topic any parent longs to hear. Aunty raises an eyebrow at my Uncle and puts her hand on his. It's time to reassure them that Wai and I are just friends.

"Wai is strong, brave, and an excellent cousin. You must be proud of her, and I'm not surprised many men compete for her attention. She'll make a great match and bring many riches to your village," I say. "Perhaps, if you're prepared to wait, when I return to Aotearoa, Starman and Marama may find a suitable man for Wai."

I flavour my words with the regret I'll feel if they pair Wai with someone unworthy. However, I'm respectful and don't indicate any intention to pursue her. Uncle raises his eyebrows while considering my suggestion, but Aunty looks perplexed.

"As you know, Wai has been difficult for us. Has she mentioned a preference for any of her admirers to you?"

"No, she hasn't, but we don't talk about such things, Aunty. We've been busy surviving, navigating, and solving problems most of the time. We still don't know where Kali's kin have gone, and I promised Wai if we came home first, I would look for them. It was Kali who decided Wai must return to you rather than continue the search for the dolphins. A caring and sensible companion, Kali. Wai is blessed to have her."

There's a pensive gleam in my Aunt's eye; she's swallowed the bait and hook. She picks nonchalantly at fibres on an unsuspecting coconut while she plots.

"The ocean is vast. How will you approach the search, Kai?" Aunty asks.

"That's the problem, Aunty, knowing where to begin. We hoped the pod may have returned here, and that helped Kali's debate with Wai."

"Didn't our daughter want to come home to us?" Uncle asks. The hurt on his face is evident.

"No, Uncle, that's not it all. Wai felt selfish about abandoning the search for Kali's kin when we spent so much time rescuing her. She couldn't wait to see you. Such a sensitive soul you've raised together because Wai is thoughtful and caring," I respond wistfully. "Kali will share with me, in confidence, all the pod's fishing spots and which ones they are most likely to visit this season.

It's an imperfect method, but Kali has to decide whether to come with me or stay with Wai."

"Oh, I imagine she'll want to come," says Uncle.

"It'll be easier if Kali comes because she can communicate with her kin over distance, but remember Uncle, that Kapanval separated Wai and Kali. It was a stressful time for them. Their bond is a gift, but it can also cause trauma when you are apart."

"Of course, you understand them perfectly. But Kai, you could wander the ocean for many seasons without finding the dolphins," Aunty comments.

"That's true, but I promised Wai I'd search for them," I shrug.

"I feel we've heaped task after task upon your young shoulders, Kai," Aunty frowns, "how will we repay you?"

"Your Aunt is right, Kai. You arrived as a guest, and we sent you into danger to find and rescue Wai. Now, Wai has made you promise to go on another quest," Uncle mumbles rolling his eyes. "We love our daughter, but we've spoiled her. She shouldn't have asked this of you."

"Ira and I are fond of Kali, Uncle, and I can't take back my pledge."

"Aue!" Uncle sighs, "is there anything we can do to help you? What would make this impossible task easier."

"I don't want to ask too much of you, Uncle."

"Ask, boy. Your Aunt and I owe you everything. How can we help?"

I still hesitate and swallow. My Aunt's eyes light up, and she snaps her fingers.

"If you take Wai and Kali, the search will be easier for everyone. That's it, isn't it? But you don't want Uncle and me to be apart from Wai again."

Reluctantly, I nod and spread my hands in a gesture of helplessness. I compliment Aunty on her perceptiveness but explain I won't ask them to give up Wai. Uncle embraces me, pats my back, and summons a woman to massage my tense muscles.

As we depart, Wai peeps around the corner and raises her eyebrows at me. I smile, hold my fingers to my lips, and look heavenward. She frowns in response, clearly expecting an immediate result. Later she told me what she'd done.

Wai marches into her parent's whare, wearing her sunniest smile, and hugs them long and hard. They are delighted with such a display of affection. It reminds them of when she was young, and it's the beginning of Wai's charm offensive. She considered all options of how best to aid me in winning over her parents when she couldn't sleep. They might beg me to take her if she's petulant and grumpy, but experience has taught her that sweetness is the way to her parent's hearts.

Aunty and Uncle wanted to hear parts of the story from Wai. She exaggerates my heroics, plays down her waspishness, and drops subtle hints that I'm a man she admires. They cry again. The thought of losing Wai is too much for them, and more hugs ensue.

Quizzing Wai on Kali's plight and the effects of losing her kin deepens Uncle and Aunty's understanding of

Kali's selfless decision. Uncle chastises Wai for making me promise to search for them after everything I've done.

Wai is contrite but insists Ira and I have the best chance of finding Kali's kin. She starts to cry, then sobs, that she must convince Kali to leave her and seek the pod with me.

"I want to go too," she sniffs, "but I know you want me to be matched and give you grandchildren. I've been selfish, but I'm scared of losing Kali, and Kai, while I sit at home in comfort."

A fresh fall of tears, hastily wiped away, wrings her parents' sympathy. They comfort Wai, who is genuinely distressed at the prospect of separation from Kali, being left behind by me, and her parents choosing a man she doesn't want. And, of course, she'll be deprived of my company – I tease her later that my departure was the cause of her tears which earns me a slap.

When Wai leaves her parents' whare to swim with Kali, they have a lot to discuss. Aunty proposes they let Wai go on the expedition to find the dolphins. As much as it pains her to be parted from her daughter again, she's hopeful that Wai and I may get together. That would solve their problem of getting Wai to choose a man. Uncle agrees because they owe me Wai's life. The thought of me spending my life adrift on the oceans when I risked my life to do their bidding isn't sitting well with him - he's an honourable man. The decision is agony, but they trust me to return after the daring rescue and destruction of Walu.

They decide to let Wai accompany me. I'm summoned once more to Aunty and Uncle's whare, where they lay out coconut cakes and flower nectar tea.

"They are sweetening you up," chuckles Nani.

She's right, and I conceal a grin behind my hand as I cough. My hosts look crestfallen but resolute as they deliver their daughter into my hands.

"I know this isn't easy for you, but I promise to work swiftly. You know I'll guard Wai with my life."

"We know, Kai. That enabled us to make a logical decision," Uncle sighs.

"Please find the dolphins, Kai. I'm afraid Wai will descend into grief with Kali if she loses her whanau. If you agree, we'll tell Wai, who has already expressed a desire to go."

I nod in agreement and embrace them, acknowledging their bravery as parents. The sooner we leave, the better it'll be for all involved.

"Can't wait to be alone again?" laughs Ira.

"No, Ira. I need to get the job done before Aunty fades away. Honestly, I'm afraid to be alone with Wai after the kiss. But, excited as well. Aue! Sometimes I wish I was a whale."

The laughter bubbles through me again, a curious sensation that's tickled me from birth.

My preparations go well, and I complete karakia with care. Tūātea is gleaming and reaching for the waves, and the villagers stow or ready supplies. The thrill of adventure invites butterflies to dance in my stomach, or is it Wai, I wonder? I sing as I work, and children arrive to dance and join in.

Wai runs down the beach, waving her arms in the air and squealing like the children.

"They said yes, Kai! I can go with you and Kali," Wai shouts, breathless from her sprint.

Her enthusiasm makes me grin, and Wai almost knocks me over, launching herself to hug me. The embrace is fierce, squeezing the air out of me. Wai is a powerful girl, and Marama flashes through my mind. I close my eyes and enjoy the sensation of being hugged by Wai, admitting I've fallen under her spell. She leans against me, nestling her curly head on my shoulder until the children's giggles break us apart.

Extricating myself from Wai, I hold her at arm's length.

"Did you doubt me, cousin?" I ask.

She lowers her eyes and nods before throwing back her head to laugh. Slapping her back, I urge her to organise the last items, and she runs off with purpose. Kali is porpoising in the lagoon because we're excited to have Wai on the mission.

There'll be a feast, but early, as we leave before dawn on the morning tide. The moon and stars will be visible, which is perfect for navigation. Ira enlists the help of the whales and Kali, the dolphins. Nani moves through the spirit world with our ancestors, looking for news, prophecies, and information. I entrust our passage to the Gods and the stars, feeling the spiritual tug. There's a reason we're voyaging, so I put my faith in destiny's hands.

Wai spends the feast with her parents, fetching them food and cuddling them like a child. They've delivered her desire at a high personal cost, and Wai lavishes them with love and attention in return.

I drum and dance with the men, sing with the children and avoid unattached women like off food. There are disappointed faces among the girls and young women, but I don't want to be on a waka with Wai in a mood. Our relationship has improved, but Wai didn't get a new personality. I need rest, so I retire early and go to my mat alone.

Darkness blankets me, and the whispering echoes, rising in volume as voices join in – then silence. A familiar presence reaches for me.

"Kai, it's Manaia. Continue to follow your instincts. The girl's heart lies where the dolphins dwell, and her life opens before her and for you. Your fate pulls you in the tide."

Sitting up with a jerk, I'm clammy with sweat, and the words of my tipuna reverberate in my head. My breathing is erratic, and I calm myself, inhaling and exhaling air.

"Nani, are you there?"

"Yes."

"Did you hear Manaia?" I ask.

"No, mokopuna, her words were for you. My grandmother seeks information on my behalf for you."

I repeat the words to Nani.

"What do they mean, Nan?" When she doesn't respond immediately, I guess, because she's been teaching me to interpret messages – an imperfect and tricky art. "It sounds like I'm doing what I'm supposed to, and finding the dolphins is important for Wai and me. She'll find her heart, and the journey is part of my fate?" I ask.

"Well done, Kai. That is as good an interpretation as any," she chuckles. "For now, you know your course is true, and finding the dolphins is significant in your lives. Other's hands weave the strands of fate, and we don't always perceive the pattern until they are almost done. Po marie (goodnight), Kai."

Knowing I'll get no further clarity, I shrug my shoulders and go back to sleep. Ira takes me with him into the deep, where I'll have peace.

Chapter 21

Seeking

Tearful faces line the shore as Wai, and I sail away with Kali playing in the bow wave. We feel guilty because the exhilaration of returning to the water and voyaging excites us. When the sun rises, I take our bearings, and the island is far behind us. Our smiles and singing broadcast our happiness to the sea as we fall into the familiar routines of sailing together.

Tūātea flows with the winds and currents, following the path written in the stars, and I'm surprised it takes Wai so long to ask where we're going.

"How do you know which way to go?" she asks.

"I put my trust in Gods, tīpuna, and the stars. You must have faith in me to jump on a waka with no destination," I tease.

"Yes, I have faith in you, but I also trust Kali's instincts which I share. She believes we're going in the right direction, and my intuition agrees. I can't explain it, but I feel

I must, no more than that – something compels me to travel in this direction with you," she frowns.

Kali and Wai's feelings underscore mine, and that makes me happy. We eat, and I fish, with help from Kali, for our next meal because I'm craving fresh raw fish. I urge Wai to nap as she barely slept to maximise time with her parents and whanau, and to my amusement, she's snoring gently in no time. I marvel at our compatibility compared to our childhood squabbling. Now I know she was just trying to get my attention; her behaviour makes sense to me. She looks so sweet and lovely, napping on her mat next to mine, and maybe I'd be content to voyage together forever.

I blush but don't know why I feel so – awkward. We're no longer children, but apart from the occasional hug and the kiss on the beach, we've maintained our distance. To keep my mind off questions I can't answer, I return to the comfort of my paddle and immerse myself, melding with the ocean.

There's a delicious tension between Wai and me. We exchange smiles and glance at each other when we think the other isn't looking and enjoy the journey. The sun rises and sets, and we take turns sleeping and manning the paddle, telling stories, and eating together. Our relationship returns to platonic cousins, but there's an undercurrent like the hidden flows in the depths. I'm patient and older, so I wait.

After several days at sea, as the sun reaches its zenith, I ask Wai to take charge while I get some sleep. The weather is kind to us, and Kali chittering alongside our waka lulls me into a restful doze.

The lurching of the waka and Wai's screams woke me. I know something is wrong, and my skin tingles as Nani, Tane, and Ira rush into my conscious, overwhelming me. Shaking my head, I focus on Ira before expanding the spiritual senses to accommodate Nani and Tane.

"Swim, Kali, swim," Wai shouts. "Save yourself," she screams as tears roll down her face.

The waka is jerking from side to side, threatening to catapult Wai into the water, but she holds on doggedly, bracing herself against the side of Tūātea. "What is it, Kai? The monster surrounding us?"

"I don't know yet, but hold on and stay low."

I roll on the deck to the paddle and grasp it with both hands before I dare to peer over the side. The creature is massive, a monster from the deep. It has Tūātea in its grip, and I swallow as I consider our options.

"Do you know what it is, Ira?"

"Yes, but the whales avoid the beast. It has nasty poison to sting anything that strays into its path. It's an enormous colony of smaller creatures that can swallow anything in its path."

"Nani, father, do you have any ideas?"

"All creatures of the ocean belong to your sea father, son. Call on him to assist you," advises Tane.

"While you are doing that, I will sing the beast a lullaby I learned from our enemies and invite sleep and lethargy to form a blanket," offers Nani.

I relay to Ira what's happening as we speak in the spirit world so Tane can hear Nani and me. The sound of the waves fills me, and I begin karakia and communion with Tangaroa, hoping he'll hear me. I tell him I wish no harm to any of his children and ask the same in return as songs of the sea's past ebb from my lips, reminding Tangaroa of the birth of his children. I sing of the future, the deeds of the children I'll father, who will protect the whales and battle for the ocean against the evil tide.

A keening lament seeps from the spiritual realm and surrounds the waka. The sea calms and the creature slumbers, allowing Tūātea to fall to a horizontal position, but the jolt of landing catapults the sleeping Wai into the water with a splash.

"Wait! Don't jump in, Kai, or you may disturb its sleep," warns Nani.

"I can't leave her to drown Nan. I must go after her. Ira will help me."

"Not Ira, Kai, he's too large. Tane can raise her. Stings cannot harm spirits, and we move without disturbing the physical world. Take your fishing net and lower it gently into the water, and you can catch her when they surface."

I do what Nani tells me, and Wai surfaces, still sleeping and rolls into my net. No doubt put there by Tane. Very carefully, I haul Wai in and wrestle her aboard without waking her. She twitches and turns over but, to my amazement, sleeps on though she's soaking wet.

"Thank you for saving her," I whisper to Tane.

My whole body suffuses with warmth, and I feel his spirit enfold me. It's a spiritual hug and connection with the man who died before I was conceived, but we know his essence is part of me, and without Tane bringing my physical parents together, I wouldn't exist.

Nani is still singing, and I ponder how to escape without waking the beast. I look down into the water and find a colossal rainbow-coloured fish regarding me with protruding eyes. From Starman and Marama's stories, I deduce my great-grandfather has come to help me. Giving thanks to Tangaroa, I let my longest rope drift from the boat with the current. Rainbow fish bites the end of the rope and lazily moves his tail from side to side, barely disturbing the water. Slowly, we are taken by the current, gently prised from the grip of the slumbering beast. I hardly dare to breathe as, finger by finger length, Tūātea moves toward clear water.

The rainbow fish pauses, and our progress stops. It's as if it checks we aren't disturbing the water too much, and once satisfied, he tows us again. The air is heavy with tension, so I close my eyes and connect with Ira and Nani, afraid my pounding heart is too loud.

"You're out of its grip, Kai, but go quietly, and we will hold the enchantment as long as we can," murmurs Nani. I can sense the efforts my tīpuna exert in the spiritual realm.

We drift for the rest of the day and into the evening, putting distance between our captor and us. I'm silent because I don't want the waking beast to pursue us.

When darkness descends and the stars appear, a brisk wind rises. Silently as I can, I manoeuvre my sails to catch the wind. Our direction isn't important at this point, and Ira stays with me for reassurance. All I want is to be further away from the creature I don't understand.

Thankfully, there was enough sun for Wai to dry, and I didn't have to undress her. I rub her limbs and cover her with a cloak to keep her warm. Kali returns to our side once it's safe. I assume Wai is enjoying dreams from Nani's enchantment lullaby.

Once I'm sailing comfortably, I dedicate myself to karakia, expressing gratitude for our escape and no harm coming to the children of Tangaroa. Eventually, Wai stirs.

"What happened?" she asks.

Kali jumps in the air to greet Wai and convey what happened in the water. The whistles she makes sound familiar, and I enjoy the dolphin's storytelling.

"And I slept through it all?" I nod with a grin and shrug my shoulders. Wai feels her hair which is so thick it's still damp. "I didn't even wake up when I fell in the water?"

"No, you did not," I reply.

"Did anything happen to me? And how did I get out? Kali said I floated to the surface and rolled into your net – how does that happen?"

"That's a lot of questions at once. So, let me answer them one at a time. My tīpuna wove a sleep enchantment from the next realm to put the beast, a colony of smaller creatures, to sleep. You fell under the enchantment's spell as well. When Tūātea was suddenly released, the impact of hitting the water catapulted you into the water. I wanted to dive in but – but my spirit guardian warned me not to wake the beast. Spirits don't disturb anything physical, so you were rescued by one, rolled into my net, and I hauled you in as gently as I could."

Astonishment is written all over Wai's face as she digests my version of events. She examines her arms and legs for stings, but there aren't any.

"I must give thanks to your ancestors, Kai. Tales of these creatures are told in our village, sometimes to scare the children and make them go to bed or behave. The sea monster, we call it, for it consumes everything it catches," Wai shivers.

She marches off and sings a mournful lament at the front of the boat, accompanied by Kali's whistling. Her body flows with her karakia as Wai gracefully expresses gratitude to the spirits and Gods for saving her life. The sight of her is moving, and I wipe a stray tear from my cheek. I promised my relatives I would guard her with my life and it's a promise already tested. Wai is so vibrant and alive; the thought of losing her makes me tremble.

"It's ok little brother, she's safe, and you're free. Life is full of the unknown, and I'm here with you," says Ira.

"Thanks, Ira. Life is sweeter after knowing danger and death. I love you, and you're a good brother."

"One of us is always near, Kai. Call us in your time of need," adds Nani.

Fortified by the support of my loved ones, I turn from the dark places fate didn't lead us. There's only the here and now, and I'm starving.

I make an epic meal to celebrate that we're alive and pillage the fresh supplies from the village. Wai's hungry, too, so we replenish our energy reserves, and as she slept most of the day, she agrees to take the paddle first. I note the position of the setting sun, and as the moon rises and the stars appear, I reset the course and show Wai where to steer us.

When I lay on my mat, I reflect on how adventurous life has been since I left Aotearoa. The faces of my whanau pass before my eyes, and I realise how much I miss them - the mischief of my siblings, the quiet achievements of my father's mahi (work), and the spirituality and cooking of my mother. But they're far away, so I turn over with a wistful sigh and sink into sleep.

Days pass in a haze of voyaging bliss, and if not for Kali's anxiety for her whanau, we may have happily sailed on for many moons. During one of my naps under the shade, Ira bubbles into my unconscious mind and nudges me to wake by sharing his excitement.

"I can't be sure, Kai, but I may have found the dolphins."

"Where? How far? How do you know it's Kali's kin?"

"Oh, oh, one question at a time, little one, or you may confuse me. Let's see – the pod is approximately two days of good sailing away, and they are on your current course. My intuition makes me believe it's them, and something familiar about their whistles reminds me of Kali. Many dolphins cluster around a tiny island with a large lagoon."

"Do you know if there are people on the island?"

"I believe there are because I saw paddling waka on the water. When we are closer, Kali can confirm if they are her pod. There are so many of them that if they aren't her kin, they must know where they are."

I can't wait to tell Wai and scramble to the back of waka to share the news. Her eyes light with hope and excitement for Kali. She will relay everything I know to Kali when she returns but now clasps me in one of her crushing hugs. Tenderly, I kiss the top of her sun-warmed head, relieved my faith led us the right way.

Once again, I break away and shoo her off to wait for Kali. It's a long time since I've been with a woman, and the body contact is causing embarrassing reactions. I seize the paddle, splash myself with water, and exert myself physically to occupy my wandering mind but to no avail.

We've been travelling together a long time, and Uncle and Aunty are supportive of Wai and me becoming a couple. When I consider our age, the attraction, and how well we get along, I'm surprised we haven't indulged in any intimacy. There's a reluctance to spoil our easygoing companionship, and disagreements in a confined space like a waka are inescapable. Nani and Ira urge me to get to know Wai, so I'm content to follow their instructions.

To escape the constant ebb and flow in my head, I merge with Ira and power through the water, consuming krill with single-minded dedication. Peace and contentment prevail.

The atmosphere on the waka is taut as the wind-filled sail. Anticipation scratches at us like an insect bite we can't ignore. Kali cavorts madly, catching her companion in her nervous energy, which makes Wai frenetic and surrounds her with an attractive glow.

Tawhirimātēa and Tūātea are caught up in our mood, and we fly across the water at pace, whipping our hair against our skulls. The current, the wind, our urgency, and the universe drive us toward the dolphins, and our spirits soar. It feels so right, and there's no hesitation.

I don't neglect my duties to the ancestors and Gods. When events are going as you want them to, you must acknowledge they've heard your supplications. There are many stories of people, even tohunga, who focused on personal desires and didn't give thanks. The outcomes of self-obsession and ingratitude are varied but not positive, and they're lessons we learn as children. Lessons stay with me, and I dedicate more time than ever to karakia, songs of praise and offerings while Wai naps. My wairua pulses with the power of spiritual energy.

When Wai wakes, her eyes grow large as she perceives the colours of my wairua.

"Kai, I- you, you look, feel - wonderful," she stutters.

"While you were sleeping, cousin, I showered ancestors and Gods with much gratitude in as many ways as

I could imagine. They saved us from certain death, and now we're guided toward our objective – finding the dolphins. I'm humbled by the support we have. It confirms the importance of our mission because somehow our voyage, and we, are instrumental in the future."

"Sometimes you sound like a tohunga, but that's what spirit guides are anyway – aren't they?"

"You're right. I've learned and trained my whole life but never thought about it that way. I guess I do have some skills."

"Kai, that's the understatement of a lifetime," she giggles. "Can you think of anyone else who can do everything you have on this voyage?"

I contemplate her question. Starman springs to mind, but he can't communicate with spirits. My mother could have performed most tasks, but she isn't a voyager and, as a woman, would have been received differently on Walu, while my spirit father Tane is a spirit, so he can't walk among us. Perhaps Rongo, the chief who adopted Maui, could have achieved a result, but he isn't a son of the sea or a spirit guide.

Once I realise the most competent people I respect and look up to couldn't have matched my achievements, I feel great.

"No, I can't, Wai. Thank you," I grin at her.

We eat together, happy with our butterflies and expectations. Once my stretchy puku is satisfied, I grab some sleep. I dream I'm a small boy, holding a butterfly in the palm of my hand. It flaps its wings, unafraid of me, and I feel the sun's warmth on my smiling face. Then it flies away. My young self sheds tears, unhappy to be parted from the butterfly as it spirals higher in the sky, dancing with another butterfly.

When I wake, the dream returns to me, and I wonder if Nani is testing my knowledge of interpreting dreams again. So, I replay the dream and ponder the different meanings such a dream could have.

I take the paddle from Wai, and it's her turn to sleep, so I kiss her head in thanks before it's my time to voyage and contemplate events. Although agitated by the excitement, Wai is tired from the physical work and falls asleep quickly.

Ira finds me, and we experience the glorious ocean together as the moon throws her shining cloak over the waves. Our life together is fantastic, and if Tangaroa didn't give us a task, I would roam the sea with my brother for the rest of my life. For the moment, I forget any cares and rejoice in pleasure until Nani drops in with a cackle from the spirit world.

"Ah, you have a good life, Kai. Always remember that. Turbulent times are ahead, but you are about to see love for yourself in its first flourish. It's like watching a Pohutukawa bloom but every flower at once – magnificent! Observe everything, and learn well."

Then Nani's gone before I can ask anything, a typical spirit interaction, leaving more questions than information I observe with a wry smile.

Chapter 22

The Dolphins

The water explodes as Kali leaps into the air, higher than I've ever seen a dolphin jump. Wai claps and jumps up and down, laughing, crying, and shouting for joy. Kali has connected with her pod.

We celebrate with Kali, for the reunion with her kin uplifts them all. Wai informs me that the dolphins thought they'd lost Kali and her forever, so they drew the whole whanau together but drifted from their usual haunts while grieving.

The sea was invaded by thundering noises, evil-smelling objects, and enormous, sometimes sinking, waka that left dead humans floating on the surface. Scared and shaken, some dolphins could no longer hear the whistles and fled from the carnage.

The pod chased them to keep the group together, but when they regrouped, they were far from their fishing grounds.

Her kin urge Kali to come and join them because they've found the most beautiful place to grieve, fish, and find happiness again.

"Hurry, Kai, we must go faster," laughs Wai.

I know we're close for Kali to communicate, so I grin and coax Tūātea to racing speed because Kali disappears ahead. It'll be an emotional reunion for the dolphins, and Wai will experience it all with Kali. With that in mind, Ira surges forward to create extra current flow, and we slip-stream in his wake. Ira scouted ahead, and there's no way Kali's kin would lead us into danger, so I'm confident we're safe. My promise to Uncle and Aunty is never far from conscious thought.

Birds appear in the sky, and we grin, knowing land is close now.

"Oh, I can't wait to sleep on the ground again," shouts Wai.

"Hot food," I yell.

Before we reach the island, cavorting dolphins surround the waka. They whistle and chitter with glee and leap in the air in groups, each trick more spectacular than the last. Wai is ecstatic and dives overboard. She surfaces with Kali, astride her back in the middle of the pod. They are her whanau too, and she joins in their fun, standing and riding on their backs, or surfing through the waves with them. As a baby, Wai swam with Kali and the pod, so they are gentle but playful with their human. The reunion is as sweet as the outpouring of grief was bitter.

"Maybe you should introduce me to your whale whanau," I tease Ira.

"I swim with my brothers occasionally, but I love you best because we bonded so early. The cows and calves stick together, mostly apart from us. Maybe I don't want to share you," he laughs.

"And I love you, Ira, more than anyone. Do you think that's why I can't commit to a mate? Because I love you best?"

"No, you're human. When you mate and have off-spring, the young will be the focal point of your life. Don't forget I watched your parents raise you. However, nothing can ever replace the bond we have. I'm also responsible for raising your calves, I mean young, and who knows what my progeny will think of their human cousins," he muses.

"You're right about Wai. The more I know her, the closer we become, and- I think she might be the mate I'm looking for. When she kissed me on the beach to make the village believe we might pair, it was a sensation I never experienced with anyone else. It was like my lips were on fire, and I was burning. I couldn't sleep for ages."

"Hmmm, it's unusual for anything to keep you from sleeping," he chuckles. "How do you feel about each other?"

"That's just it, Ira. I'm still confused. We've been cousins and voyaging companions for ages, and it's still, you know – awkward."

"I'm not an authority on human relationships, Kai. Perhaps you can ask Nani?"

I let out an audible sigh. "I love my Nan, but she's a spirit, and unless we're in danger, her messages and dreams are as cryptic as they come. No, Wai and I have to sort this out for ourselves. Probably a rite of passage considering the many angst-riddled love stories I've heard."

"I'm here if you need to talk, little brother."

Talking and thinking are all I've been doing. A friendly wave splashes my face, and the answer pops into my head – I need faith. The journey has pivoted around my trust in the ancestors and the Gods. Choosing a mate isn't any different. I sing a song of praise and thank my sea father for sending the wave and the answer I sought.

An island of green, fringed by blinding white sand, awaits us. The arms of a reef encircle an enormous sheltered lagoon of the bluest water I've ever seen. Its colour is unbelievable, almost iridescent, so inviting and teeming with colourful tropical fish lazily going about their business. Out at sea, where we are, it's still deep, and the water is alive with the larger fishes the dolphins love to eat. I can see why they believe they've found paradise.

A few people arrive on the beach to watch our approach. Wai and Kali stay beside Tūātea because the sight of a gorgeous girl on a dolphin accompanying one man sailing a waka is the seed for a story for the onlookers. We must look quite a company from the shore, but it's crucial we don't appear threatening.

People seem relaxed, and children play in the shallows, splashing each other. I anchor Tūātea in the pristine lagoon and dive in to swim ashore with Wai and Kali. The water is tepid, warming my skin like the mineral pools in Aotearoa, and to my surprise, the tiny fish aren't afraid of Kali or us, and they surround us in darting clouds. I share my experience with Ira, whose blubber trembles in appreciation.

Wai kisses Kali goodbye, and we emerge in unison from the water. The children become quiet and shy, hiding behind bemused but smiling parents. An older man and woman step forward and place strings of shell and polished coral around our necks in a formal greeting.

The man is Poi, and the woman is Tala, and they trace their ancestry back to the God of the Sea – my father. They explain their chief is visiting another island to trade and ask us to accept them as hosts in his place. I agree with them and recite my whakapapa, then Wai's, to our common ancestor and sing a song with Wai. They express appreciation for our beautiful words and singing.

An older boy and girl proffer drinks in coconut bowls, and they try, unsuccessfully, not to gawk at us as we drink. The drinks are refreshing and delicious, so Wai and I thank them as we hand back the bowls. Their faces suffuse with colour in a synchronised blush. They are on the cusp between childhood and becoming adults, and I empathise with their awkwardness.

As is the custom in the islands, they invite us to eat. I glance at the sky and see only an endless swathe of blue, so I leave Tūātea afloat for the moment. But, I ask the children and villagers to call me if the wind rises, the sea swells, or the weather changes. My waka and I have travelled many tides together, and it's my responsibility to ensure Tūātea is safe. The sailors of the village nod their heads in appreciation of my understanding of the fickle weather and ocean.

With a welcoming smile, our hosts beckon us to follow them to an open fale to dine. There are bowls of water and flowers to wash our hands, and the aroma of fish cooked on the coals greets us. My stomach rumbles, eliciting a giggle from our hostess, who passes dishes of starchy vegetables, seafood, seaweed in coconut, and more drinks. The meal is lovely, and I do it justice, amusing Wai and our hosts.

With formalities out of the way, they show us to the guest fale, and we bring Tūātea ashore. People arrive to help us with our gear, look at us and giggle. The island is isolated, and they receive few guests, so we're a welcome distraction and curiosity. We play with the children who vie for our attention, all bashfulness forgotten.

Their chief will arrive home before the sun sinks, they tell us. I'm not sure how they know, but they're certain, and our hosts advise us there'll be a feast to welcome him home. Poi and Tala extend a formal invitation, ask us to wear our best garments, and inquire if we need any supplies.

Wai wants oil and flowers, and I want to bathe so the afternoon disappears as we groom ourselves. I wash and untangle my hair, clean my nails, oil my body, and don fresh garments, and it feels good to be salt-free for the first time in days. When Wai emerges from a fale surrounded by cooing girls, I can see why – she's stunning. My mouth hangs open slackly because I don't know what to say.

Aunty packed Wai's best garment, adorned with seed pearls, mother of pearl, and stained with floral dyes and squid ink. Her red coral and shark tooth necklace identify her as a chief's daughter on their islands. I incline my head in mute appreciation of her efforts.

"Do you like it?" she asks.

"If I was blind, I would still love it – you're radiant cousin. No wonder men traversed the ocean to win your favour and heart."

My flowery words cause a flutter of girly lashes as the entourage all lean toward me. I hope Wai doesn't notice and become annoyed with me again because she can be rude, and we've just arrived. But, she's thrilled with my praise and departs with her retinue of attendants to continue her primping.

Our mats remain rolled up where we left them. The villagers haven't placed them together or apart, perhaps as confused about our relationship as I am, so I leave them till later. If a cool breeze blows tonight, we might snuggle together and – who knows?

I daydream for a time, then practice with slow movements, the fighting patterns committed to memory long ago. The old Chief, Starman, Marama, and Tane have all encouraged fitness, suppleness, and the virtues of muscle memory. On my first day here, it would be rude to take out my weapons, but I'll ask if I can practice without offending anyone tomorrow. The concentration takes my mind off the vision of Wai.

Drumbeats split the air with their festive tattoo. People head to the beach, chattering animatedly about the success of the trading, the guests, what dances they want to perform, and the food. The villagers are dressed in their finest garments and wearing their fanciest adornments, clearly ready to celebrate.

Wai and I are offered stuffed mats near the vacant seat of the absent chief, which is an honour, and Poi and Tala engage us in lively conversation. When they find out we are storytellers, and I have voyaged since I was a boy, they enlist us to entertain the villagers after the feast. The request gets Wai and me thinking about stories to tell, and we discuss complementary tales to amuse, scare and make the villagers swoon.

As the sun flames the horizon with fiery tendrils of orange and pink, the drums still, and a hush descends on the village. Tala stands and begins a chant that sounds similar to our karanga call but more melodious. Faces turn toward the lagoon, the villagers' expectations and excitement etched in their features.

My eyes search the sea, and the jumping dolphins are difficult to ignore, but as they approach, I see a man standing atop two dolphins as Wai did earlier. He's quite a sight to behold, with his long hair streaming behind him. Once in the lagoon, he rides astride one of the dolphins. The whole village rushes to meet him, and we do too, caught up in the mood.

Tala and Poi walk into the water to be the first to greet their chief and nephew. To my surprise, Wai is right behind them, but then I spot Kali chittering at her sister in the shallows.

The man who strides out of the water is a chief in more than just name. His leadership shines in bearing, his aura is magnificent, and he's as sleek and muscular as his dolphins. He shakes the water from his hair, sending a shower of droplets shining in the dying rays, and hugs his Aunt and Uncle.

The words of prophecy sparkle in the air as Wai and his eyes meet.

'The girl's heart lies where the dolphins dwell, and her life opens before her and for you. Your fate pulls you in the tide.'

I watch, with the rest of the village, as the dolphin companions fall in love. They can't take their eyes off each other or let go physically. It's like they are being fused into one as the ocean flirts with their ankles and the dolphins whistle a romantic chorus of happy noise.

My heart fractures into jagged pieces, brittle with the sharp strike of loss. In a moment, the future shimmers and shifts as I consign what might have been to the past.

"I am Hoa," he says, taking Wai's hand.

"I am Wai," she says, "and I've been waiting for you."

When they embrace, the villagers cheer, and the drums tattoo frantic beats as dancing breaks out along the waterline. My smile freezes, and I'm grateful to the girl who pulls me into the frenzied dance.

"I'm here, little brother. It appears we have been instrumental in achieving someone else's match – your cousin's. Does it hurt much?"

"Honestly, Ira, I feel like someone punched me in the gut. It hurts like hell. Even worse, he is perfect in every way for Wai. Kali is beside herself, celebrating with all the dolphins. How do you compete with that?"

My question is laden with bitterness because there's nothing I hide from Ira – he's my confidant, always has been. He wraps me in his unconditional aroha as I wallow in self-pity.

"Come, Kai," says Nani gently, "you had many opportunities to win the girl's heart. Do you really believe she is the one for you?"

"We are so compatible, Nan, and she loves the sea as I do. Where am I going to find another woman like that?"

"You haven't answered my question, mokopuna – do you believe she's the only one for you?"

Nani doesn't ask irrelevant questions, so I ponder what she asks. Have I squandered opportunities to win Wai? Is she the only one for me? If she is, should I fight for her even though I can see how happy she is? Is my heart broken, or is my ego dented? – all the questions and thoughts swirl in my head like a whirlpool.

"I don't know, Nan. If I don't find anyone who understands me and I die alone, I'll know the answer is yes."

"You just witnessed two people falling in love, Kai. Did you ever feel like that about Wai?" Nani persists.

"No, Nan, we never had that kind of attraction."

Nani and Ira give me space for my thoughts, for which I'm grateful because I don't want to argue when I'm upset. They're kind and gentle with me, and I appreciate their support and honesty because the rest of the feast is a celebration of Wai and Hoa's newfound love.

I do my best to celebrate and share the new couple's happiness. Wai throws herself into a dance with me before dragging me to meet Hoa, who is charming and apologises for being distracted by my gorgeous cousin instead of observing polite protocol. I'm magnanimous, apologising that Wai has that effect and that he arrived without warning as I slap his back with a laugh. Hoa takes in my appearance. It's a measured assessment to decide if I'm a threat, competition or not – an alpha male protecting his mate and tribe.

Does he have heightened senses, I wonder? Can he perceive my wairua or aura the way I perceive his? I know I'm an attractive man approaching the prime of my life, and I am a son of the sea – what does this man think of me?

There's tension between us, and Hoa hugs me a bit too hard to be comfortable. Wai beams because she desperately wants us to like each other – the man she's fallen in love with and her adventurous cousin.

The night is painful, even after my admission that Wai and I don't have the chemistry she and Hoa have. I go to my mat alone again. Although I'm the subject of much attention from the island women, I'm not in the mood for a casual fling when there is my destiny to fulfil.

Wai doesn't join me in the guest whare until the sun makes an appearance. I know because I don't sleep. She changes into her usual attire and heads for the lagoon, where Hoa, Kali and the dolphins await them.

Last night Wai told me the dolphins have bonded with Hoa. For the first time, they understand Kali and Wai's bond and the joy it brings. Hoa and Wai have just met, but they know they're meant for each other and already share a family.

It's not in my nature to be jealous; however, I envy their easy relationship and the certainty of their love, which manifested instantly. The notion that I've missed my chance plagues me, and I may never find what I just witnessed. Even Ira believes my parents are exceptional, and plenty of couples in the village have average or un-happy relationships.

Uncle and Aunty will be delighted Wai has finally met the man of her dreams. They are desperate for grand-children. Hoa is a chief, and the island has the comfort-able feeling of wealth, although it's more remote than my relatives would like. Whether or not I'm pleased with it, I must take Hoa to meet Uncle and Aunty because I inadvertently brought about the match. Aue!

I'm tired, but I need the feel of the ocean and Ira. The swim refreshes me, and the physical exertion calms my swirling thoughts as Ira meets me in the deep, where I climb aboard his back.

Ira knows I crave release from my responsibilities and turbulent emotions, so he powers through the water with playful enthusiasm. His mood affects mine, so I'm as happy and reckless as he is before long. My cares evaporate as I accept that fate is out of my hands and Wai won't be my mate. I feel Ira's approval as my wairua returns to normal.

"Women, Ira, my father warned me to accept rather than try to understand – how wise he is."

"Your father is also smart. He knew Marama was the one, but he waited patiently for her to overcome the grief of losing Tane. Two men who loved your mother and put her happiness before their own – something exceptional, Kai. But, if I were a human man, I would also choose Marama and pursue her to the end of the ocean."

"Is that so?" I laugh.

"Yes, I'm a whale, and I'll always compete for the best mate," Ira brags with a swish of his tail.

I hang on as we disappear below the surface and enter the world of the fishes. They know Ira is no threat and dart about, curious. Years of riding Ira has trained my lungs so I can hold my breath for an extraordinarily long time, and Ira knows when my oxygen needs replenishing. By the time we surface, Ira and my sea father have restored my confidence and place in the world.

"Thanks, Ira."

"You're welcome, little brother. Remember, not every chase yields a result, but there will be other opportunities."

Safe with Ira, I nap on his back before the sun becomes fierce. When I return to the island, I'm ravenous, and the people on the beach point me to where I dined with Tala and Poi. A fine spread awaits me, and my hosts regale me with the gossip from the feast as I eat enough for three people.

Once I've licked my fingers clean, Tala indicates they would like to speak with me. I assume they will open negotiations regarding Wai and Hoa's match, negotiations that Uncle and Aunty need to complete. Tala surprises me.

"We hope we haven't offended you, Kai. Last night, you went to your mat alone. Did the girls and women of the village fail to please you? Or aren't they good enough for a whale rider?"

"Not at all." I pause, picking my teeth, while I consider how best to answer because her question is polite but loaded with the implication I've offended them. They could also place me in an uncomfortable situation to give them a negotiation advantage. Either way, I need to tread carefully.

"Tangaroa has given me a task, a significant quest, which is an honour for any man. I must focus and avoid distraction or entanglement. Your women are beautiful, and I consider them one of the most difficult tests I've faced, but I gave myself to Tangaroa to fulfil my quest. I'm a young man, so I find self-discipline a challenge."

Their eyes light with curiosity, but they know it would be rude to ask about the will of a God, and they cannot risk offending Tangaroa when they live at his mercy. I hold their gaze so they know I'm sincere. It's no lie, for I've never been celibate for this long, a week here and there for ritual cleansing but no self-denial on this scale.

Poi grunts his approval and hands me another drink. The haggling for Wai begins.

Although I'm a young man, I've experienced many negotiations when travelling and trading with my father, accompanying the old Chief to form alliances, bartering skills and healing supplies with my mother. When visiting his adopted village with Maui, I learned much from chief Rongo.

I hold the advantage. Hoa wants Wai at any cost, and while she desires him, her family must agree to the match. My duty as the family representative is to obtain as much wealth for my whanau as possible because they will be losing a daughter. The couple wants to live here with their dolphin whanau.

The extent of the island's wealth becomes evident as the day wears on. Their chief is an incredible trader who plies rare corals, mother of pearl, black pearls, artistic adornments, foraged treasure, fishing lines, and nets. With dolphins to help find what you seek and the favour of Tangaroa, the results are astounding.

Our polite but complicated dance of words lasts most of the day. We conclude with a swim and another meal. My relations will be satisfied with my efforts, and their job is to extract more. With that in mind, I've left some juicy concluding deals for Uncle and Aunty to request.

Wai returns, radiant, and runs straight to me for a hug. She searches my face, hopes written on her features because she's desperate to build her life with Hoa. I take her for a walk, as it won't be advantageous for people to see us succumbing so quickly. It's a game played hard and by the rules on the islands.

"How did it go, Kai? You know I love him, and my happiness and Kali's depend on us making a match. I don't care if they have nothing we want."

Her childish outburst cuts me. My feelings are still raw, but I ignore them and return to my duty as her senior relative.

"Hush Wai, you know better than that." I hold her by the shoulders to capture her attention. "You must stop this. Your parents will lose you if you make a match with Hoa. As your only relative here, my job is to ensure my Aunty, Uncle, and your village are in the best negotiating position possible. You saw the wealth brought to the island to compete for you, and you're the daughter of a chief. Some duties come with your position Wai." She looks so crestfallen I want to comfort her. "Trust me, ok? For a bit longer, I'm sure we can achieve the result you want."

"Oh, I do trust you, Kai – more than anyone who isn't a dolphin. Thank you, thank you, for doing the right thing by my parents and people. I know it's important, but I'm so in love with Hoa – I can't think properly."

She gives me a wan, crooked little smile that makes her look much younger. I open my arms, hug Wai and kiss the top of her head like the fatherly cousin I've become. The responsibility for her future is in my hands, just not how I thought it would be.

Chapter 23

Negotiations

Hoa isn't any more patient than Wai, and he's chief. All my requests are accepted, and we eat together and plan to present the proposition to our whanau. Wai sits respectfully at my side while proceedings run their natural course, but she and Hoa are hopeless, gazing at each other. We are almost nonexistent.

Fortunately for Hoa, Poi and Tala are paying attention to my briefing, and he tears his attention away from Wai when his aunt kicks him.

"I apologise for my inattention Kai. Your cousin has captured my heart and head," he laughs. "Please forgive me."

"Would it help if Wai wasn't here?" I ask.

"No, please, our future is important to us, and I promise to be more disciplined."

The smile Wai gives Hoa could light up the sky, and Poi and Tala pat her hand indulgently. I sigh inside, eliciting a chuckle from Ira. Thank goodness we concluded negotiations without the happy couple because they would have inhibited the process.

We decide to travel together to Wai's home, but when close, Wai and I will go ahead to prepare the village for the arrival of Hoa and his people. My astute cousin wants time to talk her parents into giving her what she wants. Wai also wants Hoa to make an entrance with the dolphin whanau, to impress people and incite curiosity. When Ira and I arrived years ago, we made a lasting impression on the villagers.

Preparations begin immediately for the voyage because Hoa and Wai are eager to depart. I excuse myself and take Wai with me so Hoa, Tala and Poi can agree on details without us. There's some niggling between them regarding the departure time and who will stay behind – family and village leader business, I decide.

An incandescent Wai skips off to the lagoon to be with Kali. Unlike me, she hasn't a care in the world, and her future is shining with promise. But this outcome is what my sea father wants, for the Gods and ancestors to have led us here. I begin the spiritual preparations for voyaging because they're more complex when travelling with other people, especially unrelated people. With that in mind, I visit the village spiritual leader to work together. We like each other, and she respects and knows many stories of the sons of the sea.

Wai and Hoa arrive hand-in-hand to help me resupply and maintain Tūātea. I'm grateful for the assistance, but

Hoa is wary of me, and I'm not yet comfortable with him, so the tension remains. The couple walks everywhere together, unable to be apart for long, and the village youngsters dream of experiencing love like theirs. There are already songs and artistic works created to celebrate the meeting and love of Wai and Hoa. Occasionally, I have cold ashes from the fire in my mouth when I look at them, but I'm also happy for Wai.

Nani recommences my dream-walking in the spirit world to distract me, and I learn many new skills. When I'm not studying with Nani, Ira takes me on underwater adventures to explore the fissures in the earth where the Gods create new life.

I study the moon, stars, tides, Gods, and ancestors to choose an auspicious time to depart and I consult with Hoa. He's impressed with my knowledge and reasoning, so we agree on a tide and course. Hoa's dolphin whanau scout ahead for him, but I have Ira, who has roamed the oceans since he was a calf and travelled further to check conditions.

The couple wants to be together, but it's also good form for Wai to stay with me. She's so miserable at the prospect of separation from her love that we compromise. During the day, she can travel with Hoa or the dolphins, but at night, she'll return to Tūātea to sleep. Neither of them is ecstatic, but they don't want Wai to arrive home in a compromised situation either. They must adhere to the ways of Wai's people.

I take two aspiring young navigators on board to teach them skills and to man the paddle when I rest, so I'm not reliant on Wai. Marama enjoys sharing her knowledge, and I do too. My companions are keen to do everything, so the journey is quite relaxing, and I nap and fish at leisure. We keep the other waka in sight, and when we are close, I see Wai and Hoa – they adore one another.

"One day, that will be you, little brother. A cow of your own to make little calves with," Ira sighs.

Sometimes, I think he's more excited than I am about the children I'll make. I laugh aloud at his whale description and know I'm lucky to have such a good companion. When Wai and Hoa come by on their dolphins to greet us, I never feel envious because I've had Ira, my brother, from the moment I existed.

A few days out, we experience some wild weather which I love. Wai returns to my vessel as the storm threatens to rage through the night, and Kali, Hoa, and his navigators know she'll be safest with me. The tempest makes me feel alive, and as Tāwhirimātea and Tangaroa tussle, I utilise and sharpen my intuition and unity with the sea.

Grasping the taonga handed down by my navigating ancestors, I perceive the undercurrents in the depths. Great-grandfather darts in my thoughts, guiding my paddle hands while Nani whispers the wind's swirling direction from above.

The trainees are frightened at first, but I sing as the waves plaster hair to my head. They realise how much

I'm enjoying the ride and that Wai isn't afraid, so they scramble to help, knowing they have much to learn. We manoeuvre through troughs and crests, often flying through the air before surfing another wave. Taking turns on the paddle with me, I ask the boys to close their eyes and feel the currents with me, and I teach them karakia, songs, and laments.

It's an experience they won't forget, and they feed off my confidence, a steady hand, and clear instructions, grinning at me, pleased with themselves. When the winds subside, we share a meal and discuss the decisions I made during the storm.

We've lost the other waka in our fleet, but the dolphins will bring us together again, so we enjoy the remnants of exhilaration. Only Wai is pining for Hoa, but she knows he's safe because Kali and her whanau communicate during the storm.

The sun bursts behind the clouds, warming our wet skin and garments. Hoa arrives on the back of a dolphin and climbs aboard to embrace Wai and check the course with me. He joins us to eat. The boys are extra proud because they're on a waka with a son of the sea and their chief.

Tūātea hasn't deviated much, so Hoa departs to round up the waka and steer them toward us. Wai dives into the water, clambers astride Kali, and follows him. I'll check our exact position when the stars are visible and make course adjustments.

We stop on an uninhabited island to replenish our water and coconut supplies, but otherwise, we stay on course and make excellent time. Any visits to relatives, and stops for trading, Hoa plans will be made on the way home. Hoa wants to travel directly to Wai's home to conclude the matchmaking we started. I envy the single-minded determination and conviction that I never had with Wai. I concede that Hoa is a good man.

The time arrives for Wai and me to sail ahead, and the wind is fresh behind us. I try not to be impatient with Hoa and Wai, whose goodbyes stretch on endlessly until I cough to announce my presence.

"Come, Wai; it's time to go home."

Hoa kisses her one last time before announcing, "Kai, I'm entrusting you with my love and life – please take good care of her." His voice catches with the emotion of parting. "And I would be grateful if you found encouraging words for your Uncle and Aunty on my behalf," he asks with a hopeful look.

I nod and reply drily, "you will learn in time, Hoa, that Wai generally gets what she wants."

Wai spears me with a sharp look my taiaha would envy and pokes her tongue out behind Hoa's back. Once he's gone, she slaps and berates me for making her sound stubborn and willful, so I point out that her behaviour proves I'm right.

After her tantrum, our fight, and some childish name-calling, we collapse in a giggling heap. Wai snuggles against me before asking, "are you taking me home or not?"

It's my turn to shove her playfully in the direction of the paddle as I ready the sails for speed. We're a well-honed team on the waka, and soon Tūātea skims the water as we squeal at the rush.

When the stars appear, I sail on while Wai sleeps. Ira is on patrol and guides me away from rocks, reefs, and the shallow water of building atolls. Tonight will probably be the last time I journey with Wai, and the thought makes me sad. In the next couple of days, she'll belong to someone else while I continue my search for the perfect mate – a depressing situation. I suppose there's a purpose behind my wandering, and I consider what Ira and I have achieved.

Ira met the whales in Rangitāhua and successfully pursued the mate he wanted. We have banished ghouls from this realm and destroyed an evil cannibal leader who corrupted the land, sea, and spirits for his benefit. We rescued Savani, Isa, and Wai, then saved her from a blood spirit. Then we found the missing dolphins and the perfect man for Wai, and I negotiated a hoard of wealth for my relatives. It's been a fine adventure - except for the lack of success finding my mate.

"That was a big sigh, Kai. Are you ok?"

I didn't notice Wai awake, and she's the last person I want to discuss my failure with.

"Yes, just thinking and missing my whanau." Better to be truthful and avoid her question.

"I, I want to thank you. If you and Ira hadn't come to rescue me and Kali, banished that awful blood spirit and looked for the dolphins, I wouldn't have met Hoa. When we kissed on the beach that night to trick my parents, I was more convinced than ever that you were the one for me. It was- like nothing I'd experienced before. Mother cautioned me not to throw myself at you. I don't know how you knew we weren't meant for each other, but we owe you everything, Kai. How will we ever repay you?"

Her honest confession sears me, and her sincerity touches me. I wasn't mistaken about the one time we kissed, and my lips burn with the memory, yet something held me back.

"Well, let me see. You can make me delicious food and wait on me when we get home, promise to name all your children after me, tell people stories about how amazing I am-"

"Stop it, Kai. I'm being serious. My parents will ask me, and I want to know what we can give you.'

"Maybe I'll ask for you after everything we've been through."

"You wouldn't," she stammers. Her face suddenly pales in the moonlight.

"No, I'm joking. I wouldn't ask to be slapped, told off, and scolded for the rest of my life," I tease.

Wai punches me on the arm, but I know I caused it. Although I didn't want Wai and never pursued her when I had the chance, the rejection wounds me. Now Wai is out of my reach, ironically, she has never been more attractive - confusing.

"Kai! You're incorrigible. Do you want to be showered with gifts you don't want? Maybe they'll gift you a mate," she suggests cheekily. Wai waggles her eyebrows up and down, reminding me of Starman, and teasing me in return.

"Ok, ok – I didn't think of that. I'll give it some thought before we arrive. But, you are my cousin, and it was my duty to search for you – we're family."

"I do love you, you know. A girl couldn't ask for a better cousin or protector."

She wraps me in her arms and treats me to a passionate hug. I'm unsure how I resisted her charms and attention, so I retreat to my mat while it's calm and go to sleep, where I'm safe from myself.

I awake refreshed even though Nani took me dream-walking and worked me hard. Wai goes to her mat yawning, for she's become accustomed to sleeping through the night again.

When her island home is visible, Wai whoops for joy because the life she desires is closer to reality. We sail the boat together, racing onward and looking forward to a hot meal. People gather on the beach, children splash in the water, and fishing craft launch, paddling out to meet us.

Unable to wait, Wai dives into the water near the lagoon and streaks ahead with Kali as I slow Tūātea. Aunty and Uncle have no idea what's coming their way. They'll be happy for their daughter but will have to travel far to see her and any mokopuna.

By the time I trek from the beach to the open air whare, Wai has babbled the news to her parents. They look pleased but await my less emotional account of events and version of the couple's viability.

They send Wai on an errand so we can speak in peace. Wai throws me a hopeful glance as she departs. Once I share the negotiation details, Aunty and Uncle beam, especially when I outline what they should request. My canny bartering skill cements my position as their favourite nephew.

Spent and with my duty discharged, I eat, then stumble to my mat to rest. Her parents can let Wai know her dreams will come true because their happiness underscores my failure.

My dreams taunt me. I see myself repairing the waka with my children gathered around me, asking questions, riding a whale with the long hair of a girl streaming in my face, and walking to a whare with a woman outlined and waving at me. While I can't see her face, she looks like Wai.

I wake sweating and shake my head to clear the images. It's still daylight, so I head to the lagoon and plunge in, letting the water cool my thoughts and body. Lots of dolphins play there, so I swim out, hoping to find Ira, but Nani comes to me.

"What disturbs your wairua, Kai?" Nani asks.

"I dreamed of the future, Nan. In that future, I have many children, and there's a woman in our whare who looks like Wai. How can I be sure I'm not changing my fate by not fighting for Wai? Is the dream showing me what I've lost? I'm afraid, Nani. Scared I might fail Tangaroa because I search for – for the improbable."

"Dreams are not defined, Kai, but images from a myriad of possible futures. You must learn to trust your instincts and judgement - they haven't let you down yet. It's the curse of the young to doubt what the head and heart know, and that makes us older people feel better about our wrinkles," she chuckles.

If there's one thing Marama taught me well, it's that Nani is always right. Maybe the woman wasn't Wai, or those children weren't my destiny.

Chapter 24

The Match

When Hoa arrives, standing astride two dolphins, hair streaming into the setting sun behind him – jaws drop in the village. It's comical to watch people's reactions, and the consensus is that he's the perfect man for Wai, and she was wise to wait. Her wilful refusal of wealthy, powerful, and handsome men is forgotten and forgiven by the villagers instantly as they fall under Hoa's spell.

I wonder if my annoyance is what men experience when I arrive astride Ira and sweep the local beauties off their feet with my charm and storytelling.

Hoa crouches in the water to signal he's no threat and comes in peace, politely awaiting an official call of welcome before proceeding. He cuts a magnificent figure, especially when he isn't standing next to me because I tower over everyone, and he wears the mantle of a born leader. It's a tense moment for Wai, and she darts me a panicked look, but the welcome call floats through the air, and I nod my reassurance.

The confidence of a man who arrives alone to plead for the daughter of another chief isn't lost on Uncle and Aunty, and I think maybe they're as smitten as Wai. When the formalities have played out, Wai runs to Hoa, and they are a picture of contentment in each other's arms. The dolphin whanau return to the fleet to signal they may come ashore.

It's obvious to everyone that Wai and Hoa are madly in love. As the matchmaker and first negotiator, Uncle and Aunty invite me to the initial interview with Hoa and his whanau. It's a formality to cement the arrangements discussed, ensure there's no misunderstanding, and get to know one another.

Tala represents the family, the tohunga Hoa's people, and the dolphin whanau, his connection to Wai, Kali, and Tangaroa – an effective delegation. They discuss whakapapa in detail to find common ground, and Tala tells the story of how Hoa came to lead the village.

Many years ago, Tala's sister, Hoa's mother, disappeared. The villagers and whanau looked everywhere for her but found no trace and mourned her loss. A cycle of life passed; Tala and Poi produced no children, and Tala's father, the village chief, grew old. Tala and Poi took on more responsibilities as the village leaders but were distraught that they produced no children to pass on or share their skills with.

One day they were on the beach together, Tala crying and Poi consoling her, when two children swam ashore and approached them. They didn't recognise the children, who were only a few seasons old, and weren't from the village. Their appearance was unusual but strangely familiar as well. The girl stepped forward.

"Your sister, the one you thought lost, sends her greetings and wants you to know she's well and happy. She gifts her son to you so that you may know the joy of motherhood, and her people have the leader they need."

The children embraced Tala and Poi before the girl kissed her brother's head and returned to the ocean. They realise Hoa has a dolphin companion when it comes to the lagoon and waters around the island, and Tala and Poi raise the boy as their own, lavishing him with love while his grandfather fills him with knowledge and wisdom.

"Did you find out what happened to your sister, and did Hoa's sister come back?" asks Aunty, intrigued.

"No, we never saw my sister again. Hoa told us she lives with his father, and he visits her with his dolphin, and we haven't met our niece again," she sighs.

"Still, Hoa is a blessing for us. Leadership sat lightly on his shoulders from the beginning, and we're grateful his mother sent him to us," says the tohunga.

Aunty is delighted there's an entertaining story to share in the evening and that Wai has chosen an extraordinary man. Wai is oblivious to her mother's approval because she and Hoa are occupying their private world again, so I guess they communicate as they do with their companions – interesting. Unusually, Hoa bonded with many dolphins, and I wonder about his parents.

The feast to celebrate the union of Wai and Hoa is lavish. Although the happy couple refuses to wait for weeks until their relatives can be invited and travel from afar, the food and entertainment organised by the village are stunning.

Uncle and Aunty are ecstatic, and their excitement whips villagers and visitors into a frenzy. The joining of a couple is a special occasion, more so than usual when it's the child of the leaders and a chief. Wai's parents spare no effort to impress their new relatives.

Hoa and Wai ask the dolphin whanau to perform a spectacular display of tricks for the crowd, ensuring their union is a day everyone will remember. The children's clapping, whistling, and exclamations grow big smiles into cheek-aching grins.

As the entertainment ends and the tohunga finishes karakia for the feast, a hush falls over the village.

There's tingling inside my body and the touch of a presence in my mind.

"What is it, Ira?"I ask.

"It's another whale, Kai, reaching out to us and- oh. Better keep your eyes on the lagoon, little brother."

Ira sounds perplexed, so I do as he asks. The approaching whale leaps in the air and splashes its tail in a playful greeting. She's definitely a female teasing me.

Great, two whales to make fun of me, I think, shaking my head, trying to dislodge the thought.

People drift toward the lagoon again, and I can't see, so I stand and follow them. Someone is swimming from the reef into the lagoon.

Hoa strips off his finery and dives into the water, whistling to his first dolphin companion. Once Hoa is astride, they dash toward the swimmer, porpoising through the water, graceful in their unity. He pulls the swimmer onto the dolphin behind him.

My heart is pounding, and I'm uncomfortably hot. It's warm, but I'm sweating, so I splash water on my face. The riders tumble into the water, and Hoa emerges with a toothy grin and runs to Wai, pointing excitedly at the rescued swimmer.

When the swimmer reaches the shallows, she stands and tosses her head, just like Hoa did when I first saw him. The same arc of rainbow-tinged droplets streams around her.

I freeze, transfixed. Breath held in my lungs, my wairua expands to meet her. Our eyes meet, drawn to each other and the exclusion of everyone else. I forget protocol and wade out to meet her, and she comes to me first, claiming my fluttering heart with her smile. She takes my hands in hers. The eyes that look into my soul are startling, the blue of my beloved ocean.

"I have come for you," she says.

Momentarily, I lose the ability to speak and I'm drowning in her eyes. My mother, Marama, has green eyes, and mine are light in colour, but I'm mesmerised. Then I realise she's still smiling, and her lips don't move – yet she speaks to me.

"Yes, we can speak as you do with Ira."

My whanau and Hoa come to my rescue.

"This is my sister, Kailani," Hoa announces.

Wai is the first to hug her new sister, also ignoring protocol, then my Aunty and Uncle, and finally, me.

It's the strangest sensation as our spirits and bodies merge – as if we always missed the other part of ourselves. We laugh at the effort it takes to let go of one another, but Lani, for that's the name she uses, must meet the other leaders.

Her name is the same as my grandmother, and her eyes are as unusual as Marama's. Lani rides a whale and speaks the same language as Ira and me – she is the perfect woman and the mate I've been seeking. I laugh aloud because after all my efforts, she found me, and people shoot amused glances in my direction.

"While Lani is busy, my name is Susi, her companion. Once she returns, I doubt I will get your attention again for some time," she laughs.

Her laughter has a similar effect to Ira's, but the bubbles percolating through my body are smaller. My manners recover from the surprise as Ira chuckles in the background.

"I'm pleased to know you, Susi – what a privilege to make your acquaintance."

"Goodness, you are lovely. No wonder Lani wanted to find you. Such a beautiful aura, and your manners are impeccable," she says.

"Oh, just wait until he curses on his waka, picks his nose, and behaves like a lout," Ira teases.

"Ira, that's not very complimentary. Don't listen to him, Susi; he's rude," I respond.

"The two of you are funny. I imagine we'll raise a merry little pod," says Susi.

"Where are you from, Susi - I don't think I've seen you before, but forgive me if I'm mistaken?" asks Ira.

"I come from the north. My family was chased and hunted so often that we almost disappeared. We decided to swim south to find a more peaceful life, and that's when I met and bonded with Kailani. A tiny predator swimming in the ocean. The other whales feared her, but now they know her and that she's my companion. Not all humans are the same."

"They are coming here more frequently, aren't they – the people from the north?" I ask.

"Yes, they are. We can't stop them, but some are more destructive than others," Susi shudders.

Silence descends as we contemplate Susi's words which echo the predictions I've received - nothing can turn the tide.

Distracted by krill, Susi swims off to feed.

"Did you know Lani and Susi were here, Ira?"

"No, I didn't. I could feel the presence of Susi as they got closer, but I had no idea who she was. But I'm happy for you, little brother. Do you mind if I go and feed with Susi and get to know her better? Once you and Lani are together, I'll need other company for a while."

Ira is right. Lani breezes through meeting the entire village in an economical amount of time and returns to my side. Hoa and Wai exchange knowing looks because they've been through what we're experiencing, and the bond is intense.

Lani is beautiful. Standing almost as tall as her brother, Lani is curvaceous but muscular, and her hair is the colour of pale dried flax. A creature of the sea like me, her skin is tanned, but it's much lighter than mine. I'm completely captivated by her, as she is by me.

The rest of the feast passes in a blur, and Lani and I remind each other to speak out loud occasionally and to other people. I feel guilty that I pay no attention to Wai, but she winks at me and rolls her eyes because she's not doing much better.

One of Lani's charms is a wicked sense of humour, and she also has a keen wit, so she entertains me, absorbing my attention. Our banter and flirting continue throughout the feast as we grow closer.

Unlike the pomp and formal ceremony of Wai and Hoa, Lani claims me. There is no negotiating, posturing, or need to please relatives. When the dancing displays end and everyone joins in, Lani and I dance together in joyful abandon, celebrating until she pulls me into the palm shadows. She places her hand to her lips, and we steal away to a deserted beach.

At first, we hold hands and let the water lap at our ankles, eyes closed – listening. Then we hear it. The sweet sound of whalesong reverberates through our bodies until we tremble. It's the mating song.

Ira and Susi serenade us as we wade into the water and consummate our love.

The intensity of our passion devours us, and when we join, I'm unsure if we're humans or whales. I am Lani, she is me, and we mesh together like two halves of a fractured coconut. After our first coupling, my body shudders with ecstasy.

Lani takes my face in her hands and trails kisses from my face to my throat, igniting fire on my exposed flesh. Her appetite is voracious, and I thank everyone I can think of for delivering her into my life.

When our bodies demand rest, she leads me to her mat, announcing to everyone that I'm her man and she's now my woman. I find her assertive assurance wildly attractive, and as she snuggles her body against mine, Lani makes me the happiest man in the ocean.

"We have created a child, Kai. I feel the stirring inside me, and so does Susi," she whispers.

"Oh my love, that's wonderful," I whisper back. "Is it still ok to practice a bit more?" I tease.

"Yes, yes, yes," she giggles, "it took me long enough to find you."

Before the sun kisses the horizon, I go to the sea and perform an intricate karakia of thanks. I open my flesh and drip blood into the sea to let it mingle with the salty home of Tangaroa.

"Your task will be done, father. The mate you sent me is a worthy mother of our ocean guardian dynasty, and we swear to protect you through generations untold."

Ira and Susi breach in unison as Lani approaches the beach behind me. Lani starts to sing, and her voice is ethereal, part human, part whale with the whispering lilt of wind, and when she raises her arms, fish begin jumping in the air from the ocean. We embrace, savouring the magic of the moment, and watch the sun usher in a new day.

Wai and Hoa appear in the lagoon riding their dolphins, looking as sleep-deprived and love-struck as we do. We hug each other, acknowledging our shared happiness.

"Had a nice night, brother?" Lani asks as Wai blushes.

"I'm sure it was as quiet and dull as yours, sister," he laughs.

And so the teasing starts and continues as we take food together, just the four of us until our laughter draws curious villagers. I tell them the tradition of my mother's home island to make fun of a new couple. That isn't a good idea because people decide to make me feel at home by continuing the tradition. Aue!

The days with my relatives, Wai, Hoa, and Lani, are moments to treasure, and my love for Lani expands in all directions swallowing me whole.

"I told you," said Susi.

"Yes, you did," grumbles Ira.

One night as I'm dreaming, I find myself sitting in a tree with Nani.

"Your patience has been rewarded, Kai. What have you learned?"

"That prophecies come true, but may or may not prepare you for the outcome. To have faith in my instincts, intuition, ancestors, the Gods, and most importantly myself."

"Sage learnings mokopuna, there are testing times ahead," says Nani.

"Anything I need to know about Nan?" I ask.

"All in good time. For now, grow your family and take Lani home to Aotearoa. Marama and Aroha can't wait to meet her."

"I'm never going to have any surprises or secrets from those two, am I?"

"Your mother once made that complaint about me," she chuckles. *"They aren't aware of the child yet because Lani and Susi are protecting her, but she'll be one of us – a healer and spirit guide."*

"I know this is a dream, Nan, but I still feel happy."

The tree fades away, and I slip back into sleep but remember the dream as soon as I wake up.

I stroke Lani's puku and whisper, "our daughter should be named Manaia if that's ok with you."

"Hmm, I adore that name and had already chosen it to propose to you," she says, rolling over with eyes closed and pulling me closer.

"It's time to head to Aotearoa. The currents and winds are turning; stars call me to voyage, and Ira and Susi dream of southern waters. I can't wait for you to meet my whanau – they will love you, but not as much as me," I breathe, kissing her.

"We are ready when you are, my love," she sighs.

Chapter 25

Homeward

Saying goodbye to people you love is never easy. Aunty sheds a pool of tears on the day Lani and I depart, and so does Wai. Even Uncle is unusually blinky. Hoa and Lani embrace fiercely but know they'll meet again when the season turns, so their farewell is less emotional. My relatives don't know when they'll see me again, and they know Wai will soon depart.

Tūātea is laden with gifts, many for Lani. When Aunty and Uncle asked what they could give me for my daring rescues, thanks to Wai, I had thought about it. Lani is the proud owner of pearls, adornments, and ceremonial garments, and I have oils, tools, spare sails, and an intricate tāmoko depicting the rescue of Wai. It's a great honour because Aunty and Uncle commissioned the finest artist in the region to complete the work.

The rich rewards make the whanau feel better, but they confess tearfully they'll always be in my debt, so before we leave, I ask for one last favour.

"Anything, Kai. You can ask for anything in our power to give you," says Uncle.

"Will you offer sanctuary and support for my descendants? The children Lani and I raise will be the first protectors - guardians of the ocean. The task was given to us by Tangaroa."

Uncle looks thoughtful before nodding his assent.

"Our livelihood depends on the sea, Kai. Your mission is for the benefit of all who live on the islands. We agree," and Uncle promises they will pass our pact from generation to generation, chief to chief, tohunga to tohunga."

We seal our agreement with a hongi. It's my tradition, but Uncle recognises the respect and significance.

The tide is running, and we launch the waka. Lani and I are thrilled that we'll be alone upon the sea for the long voyage to Aotearoa. Ira and Susi relish the prospect of travelling as a family. Their instincts are urging them to go south.

Children and villagers sing as the waka shrinks to a dot on the horizon. They're sad to see us go because we've contributed much entertainment to otherwise routine lives. Their stories are enriched, supplemented by the tales we shared.

But, at sea, we are free and in our element. The wind smiles upon us, filling our sails while the sun warms our skin and days. Lani and I explore each other's body, mind, and spirit – marvelling that we can never get enough of each other. We cuddle up to sleep against whoever is on the paddle, unable to be parted for a moment.

Lani entrusts me with her story, and I reciprocate with mine - shared secrets that meld us closer together. Our excitement grows with the baby in her puku as we share dreams and hopes for the future. I anticipate the day we disagree and argue like Wai and I did when we voyaged, but it never comes because we're so compatible, anticipating our partner's needs.

Rangitāhua beckons us ashore, and we spend magical days exploring the island and sleeping in the cave where my parents pledged themselves to each other.

I copy Starman's preparations to create a romantic setting for my woman. Crystals twinkling in the light fascinate Lani, and we bind ourselves with pledges. Afterwards, our lovemaking is slow and tender.

When Starman first approached me about learning the art of sensual pleasure, I was embarrassed because none of the other boys' fathers spoke of such topics. But when I became interested in girls and women, I appreciated my father's advice. Like Ira, in Starman's village, men competed for a beautiful and fertile mate, so I was lucky I learned how to give pleasure in many different ways. I attract women like a flower seduces bees, thanks to Starman.

My tīpuna visit us and bestow gifts upon the baby just as I received the knowledge of ancestral navigation in the cave. We can tarry longer in this spiritual place because Ira and Susi must voyage in season, and they're late travelling south.

Home is calling me, and I dream of Aotearoa. The mists cloaking Papatūānuku, fish running in rivers, the moody colours of the sea, heaving and swelling, and the towering snow-capped mountains. Lani has never ventured this far south, as she and Susi usually separate for a few months, as Ira and I once did.

"I believe you will like Aotearoa Lani. It's a spiritual place and vast. Islands are so large it takes many days to travel around them, and the western coast is wild with storms but magnificent. My whanau live on the East Coast, which is warmer, but you may find the temperature cool," I warn.

"Tell me more, Kai. I want to know about your whanau. I'm aware that I am, well, unusual to look at. My reflection in the rock pools is different from everyone else I see. Do you think they'll accept me?"

When I imagine my mother, the urge to laugh bubbles inside me, but I suppress it to reassure Lani. It's the first time my confident love has expressed any concern, and it's regarding how she'll fit into my family. I'm touched that Lani wants my whanau to accept her.

"They'll love you because I love you, but also for yourself. In my family, nobody is ordinary. My mother, Marama, is just as unusual and charismatic as you are, my love. People stare at her wherever we go until they're used to her. My father is also a son of the sea - taller than most people and still handsome." I waggle my eyebrows at her to imply I'll remain good-looking when I'm old. It makes her laugh.

"What about your siblings? Will they be jealous I've stolen their brother's heart?" she asks.

"My siblings are pretty unique. Aroha has been a spirit guide and healer since she was about four seasons, so she'll know about you already – and she always wanted a sister. Then there's Maui, destined for a turbulent future and to unite the tribes against a common foe. To be honest, I'm more worried about us scaring you off," I grin.

Lani learns as much information about my whanau as possible.

"You love them, don't you," she says.

"More than anything except you," I reply. My eyes become misty with tears. "I can't wait to see them again, hold Aroha, play with Maui, and be hugged by my parents. They're going to love you. That's what my whanau is about – aroha."

Lani snuggles against me, more content now she's prepared. I admire her research and caution and believe she'll be a fiercely protective mother. I start daydreaming of the children we'll have.

"Do you think any of our children will have your hair colour?" I ask. "I bet at least one of them will have strange but beautiful eyes like you and Marama."

We spend the rest of the afternoon speculating, laughing, and imagining our future together. The weather is mostly good, with an occasional squall, allowing us to harvest fresh water, and we almost don't want our journey to end. We know we're close when large seabirds appear, and the clouds hug the land mass.

Ira returns to the waka to guide us to Kāingatipu at night when nobody else is upon the sea. We don't want any delay or confrontation with people who might be afraid of Lani's appearance. Shortly after dawn, as we close in on the bay below my home, a karanga rolls from the hills. It's Aroha; I recognise her voice, but it has strengthened and echoes across two realms. The karanga isn't just voice and sound with Aroha. It fills you with the warmth of welcome – we are home.

Chapter 26

Life

Starman and Marama wave at us from the shore, and Lani turns to me, smiling. She feels welcome and has spotted my mother's red-gold hair, but I can't wait for her to see the green eyes. Lani is in for a surprise.

Maui can't wait and jumps in the water to swim to the waka as he wants Lani to meet him before his sister, and Aroha is busy clambering down the track from the hilltop. I pull a shivering Maui onto Tūātea. His eyes grow large when he sees Lani, but he doesn't hesitate to hug her, and I know she's charmed, like everyone else he meets.

Maui's wairua has attracted people to him since the day he was born. I ruffle his hair and throw my cloak around his bony shoulders. Maui does a victory dance to annoy his sister, but she just laughs – oh, how I've missed them.

There's a lump in my throat. These are my whanau, the people I love most in the world, and Lani is part of that. I feel the familiar caress of sand and stones against my feet as I wade through waves and shallows to the beach I grew up on.

Sweeping Lani into my arms, I carry her onto our sacred whenua and place her gently on her feet. The welcome party sings a song about the journey to Aotearoa and our whakapapa. Lani is welcomed officially by the leaders, as my woman, to join our hapu. It's a poignant moment, and I see my parents exchange teary looks. I hope with all my heart that Lani and I will have such enduring love.

Aroha performs the rituals of the spirit guide for practice because Marama wants to savour my return. We've always been close, my mother and I, and it's her I want to introduce Lani to the most.

The two women stare at each other. It's a quiet assessment of someone who may be more strange than they are. They burst out laughing and share a long hug. I exhale a breath of relief because I'm desperate for them to like each other.

Marama holds Lani at arm's length, shaking her head in disbelief.

"Well, Lani, you are a surprise and very beautiful. Who knew one family would have green and blue-eyed women with red and light hair? Huh!"

Starman steps forward while Marama claps her hands, still laughing, and embraces Lani.

"Welcome, daughter, to Kāingatipu, our home, and whanau."

Aroha claims the next hug, curiosity lighting her face, and I know she wants to ask lots of questions. She adheres to protocol, probably saving them for later, and I want a hug too. When we hug, our auras combine, throwing familiar hues of comfort and love. Lani notices, and her mouth forms a moue as she follows the movement. She raises her eyebrows at me, indicating her approval of her new whanau.

The old Chief, Marama's guardian, Starman's mentor, and my tutor greets me with a hongi. He has aged and stoops a little, but I love this man, and I'm thrilled he came to meet us.

Once the village leaders complete formalities on the beach, we walk up the hill together, where we're welcomed onto the marae before we go to eat.

Marama is as famous for her cooking as I am for eating, and the meal is delicious. All my favourite fare is there – smoked eel, roasted wood pigeon, fresh paua, kina, pickled seaweed, charred kumara, fish stew, and my favourite herbal drink. There's also crayfish for the Chief – his favourite.

Marama presents Lani with a raurau (woven basket) with a little bit of everything in it. She tucks in, licking her fingers and closing her eyes to appreciate the subtle flavours Marama infuses in her food.

Lani fits in perfectly, discussing herbs, remedies, recipes, and fishing with the whanau.

"May I feel your puku?" asks Aroha.

I'm glad I warned Lani Aroha and Marama would know about the baby. We exchange a look, and I nod that it's ok with me so Lani can decide.

"Of course," says Lani.

"Nani told me she's going to be one of you – a healer and spirit guide," I boast.

"Her name will be Manaia," smiles Lani.

"Thanks for agreeing to our traditional name," says Marama.

"Actually, I think she chose it because that's the name I had in mind," shares Lani.

"Oh, that's interesting, maybe even significant," muses Aroha, gazing into the air as if involved in another conversation. "What about him? What's his name?"

Marama flutters her hands and mutters to herself. "Yes, I see him, Aroha. Clever boy to hide and make his heart beat in time with hers - I've never felt anything like that. Blessed with twins, Lani. We'll have to take extra good care of you."

I blink at Lani like a fish surprised underwater, but she doesn't look any less startled than me.

"Oh, you didn't know. I'm so sorry to blurt out the news like that," Marama apologises.

"It's fantastic news," I shout.

Starman slaps my back, and we hug because two babies are an extraordinary gift of abundance. I know Marama is correct, Lani will need care, but my mother has delivered more babies than anyone I know. Lani is speaking with Susi, asking her if she knows.

"I did notice him recently, but then he disappeared again, so I thought my imagination was playing tricks on me. How intelligent to cloak himself because the young are often vulnerable," Susi says.

My mother's forehead is furrowed in a frown. "What is that? Is that your whale Lani?"

"Can you speak with whales, Marama?" asks Lani incredulously.

"Please, call me Mama. No, I can't talk to them, but Ira speaks to me, has since Kai was a baby, and there's a familiarity to the touch with my mind."

Aroha looks a little peeved that she can't speak to the whales until Nani promises to teach her.

The day passes in a haze of reunions, storytelling, and eating. My adventure is a long tale, and Lani arrived with many stories nobody has ever heard.

I notice my parents have taken over many duties of running the village while my best friend Koha is trading in the south. Hopefully, he'll return soon because I miss my friends and I want to invite Piki and his hapu for a feast.

Always a leader, Piki was chosen by his woman's people as the chief. While it's good for him and them, we miss his fun, astute decision-making, and martial abilities.

I store Lani's belongings in my whare and expand it to accommodate the family we'll soon have. We settle into the familiar routine of village life, and we're so happy together.

When Koha returns, we gather many friends and whanau to celebrate my 'Pale Whale Woman' Kailani. Legends are growing about her the same way they did around Marama.

Susi and Ira depart for the icy sea. Starman and I once went to the ice islands, and it's beautiful but too cold for me.

Our son continues to amuse my relatives in the physical and spiritual realm because he can hide from them. Nani, Manaia, Aroha, and Marama speculate about the skills he's developing in the womb and what they mean for him in life. They've already bonded with our daughter Manaia who will grow into another accomplished and formidable woman. But, try as they might, they cannot unravel the boy's future.

Starman and I are hoping for another son of the sea. I imagine us training him for his trials in the sea cave and anointing him as we were, but nothing is certain.

Lani glows with health during the pregnancy. She swims daily and plays with visiting dolphins, and her appetite remains healthy even when she complains there is no space for food. The cold doesn't bother her, and she enjoys it.

"Gosh, Kai, I am a whale, just like Susi," she giggles.

"But you are my whale darling, Lani, carrying our calves."

We giggle, and I tickle her feet until she begs me to stop. Mama told me not to give Lani any grief or frights because her time is close, so I do as she asks. There are so many instructions from Aroha and Mama that it's difficult for me to keep up. However, Lani takes in everything and follows their instructions meticulously, rubbing oils into her skin, eating particular foods at different times, and learning complex karakia. The women immerse themselves in homage to Papatūānuku, invoking her care and protection for Lani and the babies.

We're on the beach when Lani's waters break - a good omen. Hobbling to Marama's healing whare, Lani already has contractions, and it pains me to see her wince. She's a strong woman, but I understand childbirth more than most men because Marama and Aroha are healers. Most of the time, nature runs its course, but sometimes there can be complications.

I'm sweating by the time we arrive. Aroha is waiting at the door, and Marama is prepared for the birth. Usually, the women usher the men out of their space, but I'm allowed to stay and hold Lani's hand because I'm not panicked by grunts, screaming, blood or afterbirth. I will leave to perform the karakia I've prepared for this day, but for the moment, I want to be with my love.

Lani transformed my life. I metamorphosised from youth to man in a heartbeat, and now I will be the father of two children. The tingling in my body is mostly my own, but Ira and Susi arrive, creating sensations with their anticipation.

Karakia is almost complete when Starman joins me for the final ritual with our sea father. Tane's presence surrounds me, and I bask in the attention of my three fathers.

Tīpuna swarm around the healer's whare, nurturing Lani and the babies' spiritual well-being with their presence. A loud cry comes from the whare, along with a joyful shout from Aroha. In a few minutes, she emerges with my daughter Manaia and hands her to me – it's love at first sight again for me. Our wairua mingles and intertwines, knitting closely and even more intensely than with my siblings.

Marama and Aroha emerge with Lani propped between them.

"What's happening? Is she ok?" I stammer.

"He wants to be born in the ocean," Aroha shouts behind her as they stumble down the path.

I clutch Manaia and follow. They stop every few steps to allow Lani to breathe through the contractions, then hurry along again.

Finally, the women reach the beach and wade into the water. Manaia is snuggled comfortably against me, so we trail behind, not wanting to miss out on the birth of the second twin.

Lani grunts out a scream as she pushes the boy out. He floats in the water before Marama lifts him into the air to draw breath, and he does so calmly without crying.

Attached to his arm, still dangling in the waves, is a tiny octopus. It changes colour to camouflage itself, so now we know why he can hide.

"Wheke (octopus)," whispers Lani, "his name is Wheke."

The companion squirts ink, imprinting its tentacle on the boy's hand and smallest finger before disappearing. It's claimed Wheke, and the child smiles.

Spreading her wrap on a rock, Marama examines the baby, and he's a healthy, contented little boy. She scoops him up for a cuddle, but Starman, who sprinted down the path to be here for the arrival of Wheke, coaxes her to hand him over. My parents are melting.

Lani, who is being tended to by Aroha, shakes her head and shrugs. We know Marama and Starman will be no help when it comes to disciplining the twins. Efficiently expelling the afterbirth so we can place it in our sacred place, Lani and I claim our children – Manaia and Wheke.

"You were amazing, Mama," I whisper in Lani's ear.

"So are you, Papa. Can we have some more soon?" she purrs.

"Ugh, not now, you two. Lani, you need to heal, and Kai, you have to look after the babies," scolds Aroha, artfully plucking Manaia from my arms for a cuddle. Now I know we're in trouble, Aunty Aroha is smitten, and Maui is running down the beach to meet his niece and nephew.

Can life be any sweeter, I wonder?

Ira and Susi leap in the air, their joy suffusing Lani and me. They sing the most beautiful song to welcome newborns into the world and the ocean. Our little family ripples with the vibration, and I sing as I've never sung before, harmonising with Ira – brothers in whalesong.

R. de Wolf was born on the East Coast of New Zealand and is of Maori descent - Ngati Porou, Te Whanau-a-Apanui, Ngai Tahu, Ngati Mutunga. After leaving New Zealand to travel the world, she lived overseas for 29 years, returning to New Zealand in 2014. Currently, she resides in Turanganui-a-Kiwa - Gisborne. The call to write came home with her.

De Wolf writes about the issues she is passionate about — equality, women's rights, the balance of nature, and the spiritual connection to our ancestors and place.

In 2020 R. de Wolf published her debut fiction novel, Guardians of the Ancestors - Book One of the Spirit Voyager Series and short story Crushed Violet in Kaituhi Rawhiti - A Celebration of East Coast Writers. In 2021 The Future Weavers - Book Two launched in November, and a book of poems, Poetry In a Pear Tree, was published in December. A self-confessed nerd and Sci-Fi fan, The Goodness Algorithm - Evolutionary Dystopia was R. de Wolf's first dystopian novel in 2022, followed by Poetry In a Pohutukawa. The much anticipated Book Three of the Spirit Voyager Series, Brothers in Whalesong, hit the shelves in early 2023.

The Goodness Algorithm

Evolutionary Dystopia

When the head of Earth's ruling Council, Prime, abducts 12-year-old Ilya's friend, Chinta Katone, he never suspects she is a telepathic spy.

It's 2144 when genetic scientist Julia discovers her son Ilya is an Evolved Being (EB) - the product of evolution accelerated by gene selection and the instigator of a revolution. The eco-focused world appears perfect, but a dominant elite control people bred to be passive.

Ilya survives to mature and infiltrates the debauched powerbase, aided by Chinta and a network of telepathic EBs. If Ilya's efforts to create a better world fail - his family and the EBs will be exterminated.